MISS MELVILLE RIDES A TIGER

MISS MELVILLE RIDES A TIGER

by Evelyn E. Smith

DONALD I. FINE, INC.
New York

*To Charlotte Sheedy with gratitude
for her patience and understanding*

I

"How come they're givin' a party for us and we wasn't invited?" the red-haired girl demanded. She stood there, legs spread apart, swollen belly thrust forward, as if the baby were not only going to come out at any minute but come out fighting. "What's the matter? Ain't we good enough?"

"Prob'ly the invitations aɪc in the mail," said the small, dark girl who carried herself hunched forward, as if to deny her pregnancy. "Or maybe they just forgot about us. People are always forgettin' about us." And she heaved a sigh.

The other girls tittered. So the sigh had been intended as mockery, or, at least, taken as such.

Jill Turkel exploded. Although she had been working up to this, the effect was startling all the same. "Forget about you, you silly little bitches! The party's to raise money for you, so you can have a decent place to stay and proper medical care and the right food to eat until your—" she caught the eyes of the other women and amended the word she was about to use "—until your brats get here."

1

Ms. Fischetti and Lucinda Rundle were too stunned to speak. Susan Melville didn't speak, because she was too embarrassed. Absurd for Jill to allow herself to be provoked by a fifteen-year-old girl into flying off the handle like that. But Jill frequently flew off the handle—and for even more absurd reasons. And, strictly speaking, the party wasn't for the girls, it was for the building.

Ms. Fischetti gathered herself together. "Now, that will be enough from you, young ladies. As for you, Ms. Turkel, I am appalled. Talking to these poor, unfortunate girls like that!"

The "poor, unfortunate girls" burst into laughter, which did not improve Ms. Fischetti's temper. She turned to Lucinda. "Really, Ms. Rundle, if your friends are going to behave like this, I'm afraid I'm going to have to ask them to leave."

"She's not my friend," Lucy bleated. "Susan is my friend. *She's* just Susan's agent."

"Manager," Jill corrected.

"I didn't ask her to come up here. I only asked Susan. *She* just came along."

It was true: Lucy had not asked Jill to visit Rundle House. Jill had taken it upon herself to accompany Susan—"out of duty rather than inclination," she'd said to Susan when they were alone for a few minutes at the restaurant entrance, Lucy having gone back inside to retrieve the folder of Rundle House literature she had left at the table. "She would never have asked you to go up there with her, at least not right this minute, if you hadn't started talking about how little of the money that's raised at these charity affairs actually goes to the charities themselves."

"But you yourself were talking about that just before she showed up."

"That's right, blame everything on me. I was talking about that in connection with taxes, not morality. I didn't expect you to throw it in the teeth of the next do-gooder who hit you for a contribution."

"It's a worthy cause," Susan said feebly. "Rundle House, I mean."

"They're all worthy causes to you. But that's not why you let her browbeat you into going up there with her. You're going because you feel guilty about having forgotten what her cause was."

That was true—in part, at least. Susan *had* felt guilty. But not so guilty that she would have allowed herself to be coerced into a visit to Rundle House, if it hadn't been for something Jill herself had let drop in the course of the conversation, something which made an immediate change of destination seem like a good idea.

SUSAN AND JILL had been having lunch at Leatherstocking's when Lucinda Rundle stopped at their table. For a moment Susan hadn't recognized her. It wasn't that Lucy had changed so radically. In fact, she had changed less than any of the other women Susan had known since their school days, being now simply a faded, crumpled version of the child she had been. It was just that Lucy had always been so dim that no one, except perhaps those close to her, ever recognized her at first glance— far different from her sister Berengaria who, once experienced, was never forgotten.

In spite of Jill's glare, Susan felt she could do no less than invite Lucy to join them. She had already had lunch, Lucy said, gesturing vaguely toward the inner room of the restaurant, but would be happy to have coffee with them. By the time the coffee arrived, she had already handed each of them a handsome brochure heralding the hundredth anniversary of Rundle House, and invited them to buy tickets to a Gala Birthday Ball to benefit the house's building fund, at five hundred dollars each. That was the point at which Susan, instead of simply writing out a check for five hundred dollars, found herself saying, "I'd gladly give you a check for a thousand if I knew it would all go directly to—to whatever it is Rundle House is in aid of, instead of having it go to pay for fund-raisers and caterers and the museum." For the Gala Birthday Ball was to be held in the sculpture court of the American Museum, which, like most public institutions in New York City, was available for party purposes at a price.

Lucy's middle-aged baby face puckered in the way Susan remembered with dread from their early days. "Oh, Susan, how could you have forgotten what Rundle House is?"

How could she have forgotten, indeed! Rundle House—the Rundle Home for Wayward Girls, as it had been called at its inception, had been the focal point of old Mrs. Rundle's life. And the younger Mrs. Rundle, Lucy's mother, had been co-opted into serving it as assiduously as her mother-in-law, on pain of having her allowance slashed, for old Mrs. Rundle controlled the family purse strings, insofar as they were controllable. Her late husband, irked that his mother, the home's founder, had made over so much of the family's capital for its endowment, had tied up the rest of the still considerable estate in a trust, to

3

make sure that no more of the Rundle capital would go "to support a bunch of teen-aged tramps," as he'd put it.

He could not stop his wife from devoting as much of her income as she could spare—without depriving herself of such basic necessities as a chauffeured limousine and homes in Palm Beach and Long Island—to the family cause. And the younger Mr. Rundle, Lucy's father, the infamous Edmund, Sr., although not otherwise of a charitable disposition, managed to support a number of teen-aged tramps privately on his allowance until he was caught in an involvement with a girl so far below the age of consent that he was forced to flee the country. His wife thankfully divorced him, receiving custody of the two younger children, Lucy and her brother, Edmund, Jr. The older daughter, who was some years older than both Lucy and Susan and had already been thrown out of all of the best schools and most of the second-best, disappeared from the scene at the same time. It was taken for granted that Berengaria had chosen—or possibly had been requested—to accompany her father.

As to where Mr. Rundle himself had gone, accounts varied. Most likely he had betaken himself to Paris, where affluent refugees from sex scandals usually headed. But various romantic alternatives were bandied about among Lucy's schoolmates: he had fled to South America; he had entered the service of the Shah of Iran; he had repented of his sins and entered a religious order; he had not repented of his sins and had founded a religious order.

A few years later, Susan's own father had undeniably fled to South America, taking with him the family millions and some millions belonging to other people. Susan and her mother had gradually lost contact with the Rundles and most of the other people they knew. Not that they were cast out socially—a Melville would retain her social standing even if she sank into the gutter—but that they could no longer afford to keep to the same style of living as their former friends.

Still, there was no excuse for Susan to have forgotten the nature of her mother's favorite chairty. The younger Mrs. Rundle had been Mrs. Melville's best friend, so Susan had been aware of the Rundle Home for Wayward Girls even before she knew what a wayward girl was. By the time she was six or so, its name had been changed to the Rundle Home for Unwed Teen-Aged Mothers, which, although more explicit, was not entirely accurate. The home's concern was, as it had always been, with the months that preceded their actual parturition. When Susan had inquired, with youthful näiveté, what happened to the babies afterward, her mother said she had no idea. "Probably they're adopted and get nice homes."

"As nice as ours, Mummy?" Susan had asked.

"Well, not quite that nice, dear. You could hardly expect that."

"And their mummies? Their real mummies? What happens to them?"

"They probably go back on the streets," her father had said, to which her mother said, "Buckley!" in such a tone that neither he nor his daughter had pursued the matter.

NOW, SUSAN NOTED, the place was called simply Rundle House, in keeping, she supposed, with contemporary mores; for being a wayward girl or an unwed teen-aged mother no longer set a girl apart from the moral mainstream. "Of course I haven't forgotten what Rundle House is, Lucy," Susan said. "I was just trying to be—er—discreet."

Jill snorted. Jill was a notable snorter. Hers were not subtle snorts. They had been know to wound far less sensitive souls than Lucy's. Her pale blue eyes filled with tears. "It may seem to you that Rundle House has no place in today's world, but our work is more important than ever. The rate of pregnancy among adolescents is higher than it's ever been. In New York City it's fifteen percent—over thirteen thousand babies each year. It's such a tragedy—children giving birth to children, babies having more babies . . ."

"Why don't they get abortions if they're too young to be mothers?" Jill demanded.

"Jill!" Susan said. Reasonable though the question might be, it was hardly tactful to query the very basis on which the foundation rested.

But Lucy seemed unperturbed. Obviously she had heard this before. "The girls who come to Rundle House want to have their babies. And they don't know how to—or they can't afford to—take proper care of themselves. They don't eat right. They don't get the proper medical care. They—"

"I'm sure you're doing wonderful work there," Susan interrupted before Lucy could recite the entire contents of the brochure from memory. "I'll send you a check for a thousand dollars—and Jill will do the same," she added, frowning at Jill to indicate that Jill had better kick in if she valued her association with a client who brought her a very comfortable annual income.

Lucy intercepted the glance and misunderstood. "You don't believe

5

me. You think we're a—an anachronism." And, when Susan tried to protest, "All right, then, promise me you'll come up to Rundle House and see for yourself."

"I'll come up there, Lucy," Susan said. "Very soon, I promise." And, when Lucy looked skeptical, "Call me later this week, and we'll make a definite appointment. Here, I'll give you my number." She wrote it on the margin of the brochure Lucy had thrust upon her, and pushed it across the table.

Lucy pushed it back. "I already have your number. And I can see you don't have the least intention of coming; otherwise you wouldn't treat the brochure like a bunch of scrap paper."

"I knew I could always get another one," Susan said, taking back the brochure and stuffing it into her handbag. "And Jill has her brochure" —Jill held it up—"which she is going to file as soon as she gets back to her office." Jill nodded vigorously.

But Lucy would not be satisfied. "Why don't you come up there with me right now? That way you won't be able to say we did anything special to prepare for your visit."

"No Potemkin villages at Rundle House, eh?" Jill said.

Lucy looked bewildered. "What do Cadillacs have to do with Rundle House? Unless you're talking about that man who sits across the street in his Cadillac all the time. He has nothing to do with Rundle House. Nothing."

Susan tried to explain the difference between Grigori Potemkin, Catherine the Great's trusted field marshal, and Victor Potamkin, Manhattan's well-known automobile merchant, but Lucy could not or would not understand. "I don't see what Catherine the Great has to do with it," she said. "After all, this isn't Russia."

That had been a favorite phrase of old Mrs. Rundle's; she had considered it the unassailable answer to any argument, the absolute last word. Apparently her granddaughter felt the same way, because she began to gather her things together. "Let's get started. It's getting late."

"Lucy, I do wish I could come with you now, but I'm busy."

"Whatever you have to do couldn't be as important as this," Lucy persisted with the single-mindedness that had made her the hardest of her family to deal with, say what you might about Berry. "What do you have to do that makes you too busy to help the poor and suffering?"

Her voice grew louder and louder as she got more excited. Some of the nearby lunchers looked at them reproachfully.

Jill spoke slowly and clearly, as if to a foreigner or an idiot. "We are going to the Fothergill Gallery to look at an exhibition of pictures."

"Pictures! You think pictures are more important than Rundle House?" And, when it was obvious that Jill, who was only minimally less single-minded than Lucy, did, "You can see pictures any time!" Lucy's voice started to take on the shrillness that in the old days had heralded a tantrum.

"But we're expected," Susan said, conscious as she spoke that she was adopting Jill's tone. "People will be waiting for us there—the man who owns the gallery and the artist who painted the pictures. They would be very disappointed if we didn't come."

"And Andy—he's my husband—said he might join us there. He'd be disappointed, too."

Oh, he would, would he? Susan thought. And how is it you didn't happen to mention before that Andy was thinking of joining us? Suddenly the prospect of an immediate visit to Rundle House began to look less unattractive. "If I don't go up there with her now, she'll make a scene," she whispered to Jill. "It won't take long, and we can go to the Fothergill later. It isn't as if we'd promised to be there at a definite time." And aloud, to Lucy, "Oh, very well, I'll go up with you now, since you insist."

She had not, she told Jill while they were waiting for Lucy at the entrance to the restaurant, said, "*We*'ll go up there with you."

"Oh, didn't you? Well, maybe I misheard you. Anyhow, if you're set on going, I'm going with you."

So, after Lucy had reappeared and Jill had gone to make a phone call to Freddy Fothergill, during which time Lucy handed out Rundle House brochures to those sitting at the bar until M. Bumppo, as the proprietor, a James Fenimore Cooper fan, liked to call himself, politely but firmly ushered her into the street, the three ladies piled into a cab. Lucy gave the driver the address and they headed west and uptown, via a somewhat devious route, because of a water main break, which, as the driver explained, rendered a direct approach impossible. That was probably why the streets through which they passed seemed a strange conglomeration, even for New York, some elegant, some middle-class, some seedy, all mixed together higgledy-piggledy, instead of breaking down into well-defined neighborhoods.

The people they passed were a strange conglomeration, too, in all types of dress, ranging from clothes that would not have been out of place on Madison Avenue to clothes that would not have been out of place on the streets of Calcutta. What was surprising was the number of people in ethnic costume—men wearing turbans, and women in what seemed to be Islamic attire.

Susan sat between Lucy and Jill and tried to make small talk that would provoke neither of her companions. "How are your father and mother?" she asked Lucy.

"They're both dead. And yours?"

"They're dead too. What about your brother. Where is he?"

"Edmund's in Peru, been living there for years. He's in the export business."

"What does he export?" Jill asked.

"Oh, this and that. Whatever it is they usually export from Peru. He doesn't get up here very often. Too busy with his business and his family."

"I gather he's married," Susan said. "Any children?"

"Three times," Lucy said. "I mean he's been married three times. And there are children from each marriage. I've lost count, there are so many. Are you married, Susan?"

Susan started to say no, then thought better of it. Lucy's mother had tried to "fix Susan up" with Edmund when they were young. If Edmund happened not to be married at the moment, Lucy might try the same thing. "I'm engaged," she said firmly. No point trying to explain her relationship with Peter. Lucy wouldn't understand. Sometimes she didn't, herself. Jill looked out of the window and smiled.

"You haven't asked about Berry," Lucy said.

"Oh, somehow I had the impression she was dead."

Lucy gave a girlish laugh. "No, it was her husband who died. She's been a widow for almost three years now. But she still lives abroad. She's more at home there by this time."

"Good," Susan said. "What I mean is, she always said she wanted to live abroad, that Americans were so—so American."

"She has come to New York a few times on business. And she's been sorry she didn't have time to look you up."

"Really," Susan said.

"She keeps saying how nice it would be to see you again. You two were always such great friends. We must make a point of all getting together the next time she comes to town."

"That would be lovely," Susan said. "Just give me advance notice of when she's expected." So she could leave town. New York City was too small to hold both her and Berengaria Rundle at the same time.

II

"**W**ANT ME TO wait?" the taxi driver asked, as the three ladies got out of the cab on one of the side streets between Amsterdam and Columbus avenues.

"No, thank you," Lucy said. "We're going to be here quite a while."

Jill groaned. Lucy misunderstood. "You won't have any trouble getting a cab back downtown, although you might have to go over to Broadway. Cabs don't cruise here too much."

Susan could believe that. She remembered Rundle House as having been on a pleasant, tree-lined, slightly shabby street, filled with brownstone row houses and a couple of small apartment buildings. The street could no longer be described as pleasant, nor could you call it "slightly" shabby. It had run all the way down to squalid. The buildings were the same, but most of them were boarded up; and those that weren't looked as if they should have been, as much to keep whoever or whatever was inside from getting out as whatever or whoever was outside from getting in. Garbage, some spilling out of plastic bags, some completely uncontained, was strewn over the sidewalks and stoops, and cats and

9

rats were nosing in it together—an extreme example of the West Side's vaunted cultural diversity. West Side rats, she noticed, were larger and fatter than their East Side counterparts (which she had observed disporting themselves on Park Avenue in the wee hours of the morning). The trees were dead and some were gone, leaving only squares of barren earth and dog pats in the sidewalk to mark where they had been.

Yet both sides of the street were lined with prosperous-looking cars, many of them late models, though none the equal of the big silver Cadillac parked directly across the street from Rundle House. There was a man sitting in it and no wonder. You'd have to be crazy to leave a car like that unguarded on a street like this. But what a price to have to pay for parking space.

At first he seemed to be the only human being in sight. Then she saw that there were other people around; in the shadow of a doorway, three men engaged in furtive transaction; in an alley, a glimmer of movement; on a stoop a heap of rags that stirred and became a man. Or a woman. Somewhere a radio was playing rock. In the distance the rat-tat-tat of a jackhammer could be heard. Otherwise, it was very quiet. Strange for a street in New York City to be so quiet.

"The neighborhood certainly has changed," Susan observed. "I can see why Rundle House is anxious to move."

"Move?" Lucy repeated. "Who said anything about moving?"

"The brochure said the party was for the benefit of the Rundle House building fund."

"Rundle House couldn't possibly afford to move anywhere else in the city, no matter how much money we raised. We're planning to expand. If we pay cash, we can get the building next door cheap—cheap, all things considered, that is. If we wait, they'll start gentrifying the street and prices will go even higher."

The street seemed an unlikely candidate for gentrification, but Susan had seen even more unsavory places transformed into pricey real estate. At least this street had originally been residential. No zoning changes would be needed, and the West Side of Manhattan was currently fashionable. Probably Rundle House knew what it was doing.

"It isn't as bad as it looks," Lucy said.

"Maybe so," Jill said, "but I'd have to walk along it alone after dark."

"No street in New York is safe after dark. Only last year a man was gunned down right in front of my house, somebody from the United Nations, I believe, a foreigner, but still it was on Park Avenue, in the Seventies, and, if you're not safe there, where can you be safe?"

10

* * *

FOR A MOMENT Susan's breath seemed to stop. She was very conscious of the weight of the gun in her handbag. Then she relaxed. Of course Lucy hadn't meant anything personal. It was just the kind of remark anyone might make in the course of a casual conversation about crime. And Jill didn't mean anything personal when she said, "There seems to have been a lot of killings of UN people during the last few years. Did you happen to read that article about it in *Time*?"

No, she hadn't, Lucy said, seeming surprised that anyone should ask her if she had read anything. And Susan, affecting calm, said Lucy was right; there was crime all over New York, as well as drugs and corruption and something really should be done about it. "I see you've managed to keep Rundle House in good shape," she said. It was grimier than she remembered but, aside from the metal plate over the front door that bore the legend "Rundle House" in large letters that covered, she knew, the smaller letters of the original name incised in the stone, the place didn't seem to have changed since she'd last seen it some thirty-odd years before. Then it had struck her as grim and fortresslike. Today, now that fortresses had become the architectural style of necessity in the city, it seemed an attractive, old-fashioned building. If there were bars on the ground-floor windows, there were bars on most ground-floor windows these days. Rundle House stood out like a healthy thumb on that sore street, save for the brownstone on its left which also appeared to be well-kept.

Was that the building they were planning to buy or was it the boarded-up apartment house on the other side? That was in a state of advanced decay and would certainly need to be rebuilt; however, for any kind of expansion program it would obviously be the more sensible buy, since it was at least six times the size of the brownstone. Yet, no matter how much they raised from their anniversary festivities, how could they hope to make enough to cover an outlay of that size? Land in Manhattan, even in such a rundown area as this, cost the earth. Inflation must have shrunk Rundle House's original endowment over the years, yet Susan had never, since she returned to affluence, received a solicitation from Rundle House, although it seemed to her that her name was on all the mailing lists.

* * *

Miss Melville Rides a Tiger

LUCY LED THE way up the three steps that fronted the entrance. She rang a bell next to the door. A rather tough-looking young woman admitted them to a spacious lobby that was pleasant in an airy, institutional kind of way. A little too colorful, perhaps. It was a bit like being inside a kaleidoscope. On the other hand, it was preferable to the heavy dark furniture and dun draperies that Susan remembered from the old days. The only thing that she recognized was the graceful curving staircase that led up to the second floor. Otherwise, everything was different. Even the reception desk was of light-hued wood with a dark-hued receptionist behind it, the very opposite of what it had been.

Behind the reception desk were several doors presumably leading to offices. Susan could hear the clack of word processors from behind one of them. It all looked very efficient. The youngish middle-aged woman who emerged from the office marked "Director" also looked efficient, a far cry from Miss Henderson, who had reigned in the old days. Ms. Fischetti, as Lucy introduced her, and as she seemed to expect to be called—no bureaucratic informality here—smiled as she greeted them. She showed no sign of resentment at having been interrupted in her work to welcome Miss Rundle and her guests. True, this was one of the administrator's duties, but that had never stopped Miss Henderson from being brusque with visitors who arrived without forewarning.

Ms. Fischetti took them into a pleasant, almost luxurious office overlooking the street. It was decorated with a formidable array of certificates, attesting to the fact that Diane Fischetti possessed advanced degrees in sociology, psychology, business administration, and similar sciences. Miss Henderson's only qualification had been that she was a Rundle on her mother's side.

Ms. Fischetti told them about Rundle House, past, present, and future, while Lucy, who must have sat through this many times before, gazed at her with the rapt attention of someone hearing it for the first time. Jill's eyes glazed over. Finally she got up, and, muttering something about "needing to go to the bathroom," wandered out. Ms. Fischetti's voice never faltered, but her eyes followed Jill, and she cut short her speech before, Susan thought, it had come to its appointed end. "Sorry to be so boring, Ms. Melville," Ms. Fischetti said, as she got up, "but one does tend to get caught up in one's enthusiasms."

"But you haven't been boring at all. And there were a couple of questions—"

"You can ask them while I take you around the place. I know you're a busy woman, and I don't want to impose on you unduly." And she

12

herded Susan and Lucy out into the reception area, where Jill was wandering about, poking her nose into things. "Why didn't you show Ms. Turkel where the visitors' rest rooms were?" Ms. Fischetti asked the receptionist.

"Because she didn't ask me."

"The urge left me, as soon as I got up. It sometimes works that way. How come none of the girls are around? Aren't they allowed downstairs?"

"The mothers are free to go wherever they want. There simply isn't any reason for them to come down here. Those who aren't in their rooms are probably in the lounges. We'll see them when we go upstairs."

Jill was not as curious as all that. "You're not going to give us the grand tour?" she groaned.

"We really couldn't ask you to take so much time off from your duties," Susan said. "Besides, as a matter of fact, I am rather busy. We're both rather busy."

"Taking visitors around is one of my duties," Ms. Fischetti said, showing her teeth. "Miss Rundle might report me to the trustees if I failed to give you the grand tour, as Ms. Turkel puts it."

Lucy gave a nervous laugh. "Oh, Ms. Fischetti, you know I'd never do any such thing. But I hope you don't mind if I don't go around with you. I do want to get caught up on my mailing." And she plumped herself down in an easy chair covered in a cheeful Mondrian-like print, took out a pile of brochures and a bunch of envelopes from her tote bag, and deposited them on a small table, which she drew up before her.

Ms. Fischetti looked as if she did mind, but undoubtedly Lucy had been on the tour many times before. It made good sense for her to stay downstairs and occupy herself usefully. Or what seemed to be usefully. Susan wondered to whom Lucy would be sending the brochures. She hoped she wouldn't be asking her for the current addresses of all their old friends.

Ms. Fischetti showed them all over Rundle House, from top to bottom. She showed them the kitchens and dining rooms, the medical offices, the therapy room, the lounges, and the classrooms. That's right, Susan thought, the girls would be of school age. In the old days pregnancy usually meant the end of a girl's education. Now, often, it meant the beginning.

Ms. Fischetti introduced them to the housekeeper. She also intro-

13

duced them to the resident nurse and the visiting doctor, the porters, the cooks, the clerks, and the cleaners. Rundle House appeared to be very well staffed, indeed.

"They must have some endowment!" Jill observed. Susan had been thinking the same thing.

The higher they got in the building, the more mothers they saw. There were girls in the bedrooms, girls in the corridors, girls in the lounges. There were white girls, black girls, Asian girls, and indeterminate girls, all looking sleek and well-fed and well, if not always appropriately, dressed. Ms. Fischetti did not introduce Susan to any of the girls, and she did not seem pleased when some of them left off whatever it was they were doing or planning to do to follow the visitors around, apparently seeing better entertainment in them than from the television sets and radios that had been providing a rap and rock accompaniment to their tour.

Susan was surprised when she saw the mothers-to-be. "Children giving birth to children," indeed! These girls weren't children; they were fully mature women despite their tender years. If their years were as tender as purported, Jill suggested to Susan when they and their guide were alone in the library—their followers having halted on the threshold, as if a step further would plunge them into some abyss. In contrast to the other public rooms, the library looked unused, the magazines symmetrically arranged on the tables, the books in perfect formation on the shelves. Apparently the girls were not great readers.

"Oh, I think they really are teen-agers," Susan whispered. "Girls like that—girls tend to mature early these days."

Ms. Fischetti's back froze. "Well, you've seen everything," she said, hustling them out of the library. She entered the elevator, obviously expecting Jill and Susan to follow. However, several of the girls crowded in behind her, whispering and giggling. "Now, mothers," Ms. Fischetti said, "you haven't left any room for our visitors."

"They can wait and take it on the next trip," the red-haired girl who seemed to be the ringleader said, at the same time as Susan said, "We can easily take the stairs."

Ms. Fischetti emerged from the elevator, pushing the girls out ahead of her. "We will all take the stairs," she announced, and started to lead the way down.

But none of the others followed. Jill positioned herself in front of the

14

red-haired girl. Susan stopped to see what Jill was up to, and the rest of the girls halted, sensing sport.

"How old are you?" Jill demanded.

"Fifteen," the red-haired girl replied in a what's-it-to-you? voice. The smaller, dark girl at her elbow said she was the same. The others gave ages ranging from thirteen to sixteen. Only one—the one who looked most like a child—admitted to being as old as eighteen, the cutoff age for admission to Rundle House. That didn't mean they had to be lying, Susan thought. Wash the thick makeup off their faces, change the weird hair styles, and they probably would look like young girls—but still biologically mature, not children by any manner of means.

"Don't you think you're too young to—to take on the responsibilities of motherhood?" Jill demanded of the red-haired girl. Jill was red-haired, too. There was something of kinship between them, Susan thought, if only in their belligerent attitudes. Only, where the red-haired girl looked older than her years, Jill looked younger than hers. She was somewhere in her thirties, but she seemed no more mature than these overripe adolescents.

"If you can get pregnant, you're old enough to be a mother," the red-haired girl said. The other girls laughed as if she had said something witty.

"Didn't anybody suggest that at your age it would be better for you to have an abortion?"

"Ms. Turkel, please! I don't know what Miss Rundle would think if she heard you talk like that." Ms. Fischetti looked at Susan.

"Really, Jill," Susan said.

The red-haired girl seemed undisturbed. "Lotsa people told me I oughta have an abortion, but I don't want one. I wanna have my baby. I love babies. I'm gonna have lots of them."

"Abortions are murder," the eighteen-year-old declared.

The other girls snickered.

Jill swelled with wrath. It was obvious she was about to make a speech. "We must go back down," Ms. Fischetti said, desperation in her voice.

Susan placed her hand against Jill's back and applied pressure—not quite a shove but enough to remind Jill that she was there in her capacity as Susan's employee. Jill started down. The girls trailed after, Ms. Fischetti vainly trying to get them to go back by talking to them in quiet, reasonable undertones. Susan had a feeling that if she and Jill hadn't been there, Ms. Fischetti would have shrieked.

15

At every landing a window looked out on the street, each framed in colorful draperies rather than veiled by an ecru lace curtain as in Miss Henderson's day. As they passed each window, the girls would wave at the young man sitting in the silver Cadillac, and he would smile and wave back. Once he even broke off from a conversation—or was it a dispute?—he was having with someone on the other side of the car to smile and wave at the girls.

"Who is that man?" Susan asked.

"I have no idea," Ms. Fischetti said.

"He's my boy friend," the red-haired girl said.

"He's *my* boy friend," the dark-haired girl said.

Half a dozen of the other girls also claimed him as their boy friend. They were very jolly about it. It seemed to be some kind of inside joke. And singularly free from prejudice, because, while the young man was black, at least half of the girls were white.

Jill continued to interrogate the girls as the procession wended its way down the stairs. "But how will you be able to take care of your babies after they're born? A lot of you aren't old enough to have jobs. Are you planning to give them up for adoption?"

They shook their heads. To a mother, they were planning to keep their babies. It made sense, Susan thought. Why nurture a being in your body for nine months at considerable personal discomfort only to have to give it up at the end? But this was neither the time nor the place to bring that up.

"How can you afford to take care of them?" Jill persisted.

"The Lord will provide," the red-haired girl said. The other girls laughed. There were nuances here, Susan realized, that she failed to grasp.

They reached the head of the flight of stairs leading down to the lobby. Ms. Fischetti paused. "Well, you mothers will want to go back to your rooms now. This has been rather an exhausting afternoon."

But the girls showed no signs of leaving, although only the red-haired girl and her dark-haired sidekick actually followed them down into the lobby, where Lucy was busily stuffing brochures into envelopes and humming to herself. A few girls came halfway down; the others hovered at the head of the stairs. I'll bet Jill was right, Susan thought; I'll bet they aren't supposed to come down into the lobby.

Ms. Fischetti forced a smile. "I'm afraid there are a number of things I must do before the office closes for the day. And I'm sure you'll want to leave before it gets dark. It was so nice of you to come visit us—"

She was interrupted by a cry of outrage from the red-haired girl, who had picked up one of Lucy's brochures and started to read it before anyone could make a move to stop her. At least she can read, Susan thought.

Apparently the girls had not been informed of the festivities that had been planned to mark the hundredth birthday of Rundle House. There was outrage; there was explosion. Both Ms. Fischetti and the receptionist moved toward the front door. Susan and Jill were about to be thrown out. Lucy looked distressed, but did not attempt to intervene. Susan had an unworthy thought. Lucy could hardly ask her for addresses if she allowed Ms. Fischetti to throw them out.

Susan spoke quickly before the same thought could occur to Lucy. "Thank you so much for an interesting and informative afternoon." She grabbed Jill's arm and pulled her to the front door.

Ms. Fischetti held it open for them. She closed it behind them. It opened again, and the upper part of Lucy emerged. "I hope you won't let Ms. Fischetti bother you," she said in a low voice. "She's so devoted to her work that sometimes she gets carried away, and we can't afford to have her upset."

"Of course not," Susan said soothingly. "I'm sure good administrators are hard to find these days."

"I suppose they are, but her godfather is a trustee, which—"

An arm came through the doorway and hauled Lucy inside, cutting her off in midsentence. The door closed again, this time with a bang.

III

OUTSIDE IT WAS even quieter than before, perhaps because the jack-hammer had stopped. Only the radio was still playing thinly in the distance. It was growing dark. Jill shivered. "It's getting cold," she said. "I'm surprised they don't have a security guard," she went on. "Seems a place like that in a neighborhood like this ought to have one."

"Perhaps they do. A security guard doesn't have to be male, you know."

"You could be right. That receptionist looked like a pretty tough cookie. In fact, they all looked like pretty tough cookies. Except your friend Lucy, of course."

But in her own way, Susan thought, Lucy could be a very tough cookie, indeed. Like all the Rundles.

They went down the steps and into the street. "Somehow, I have a feeling you're mad at me."

"I'm certainly not pleased with you. There was no reason for you to behave like that."

"There was every reason. You know what those girls are—whores!

And that's their pimp, sitting across the street, protecting his investment."

"I got the impression that he was a drug dealer."

"The two occupations aren't necessarily mutually exclusive. Anyhow, with a lot of his girls off the street, he probably makes money any way he can."

"But what makes you so sure he's a pimp?"

"I recognized him. His pictures were in the papers a while back. Not the kind of papers you read. The tabloids."

She overestimated her client. Or underestimated her. Susan did read the tabloids, but her interests were very specific. She ignored everything that lay outside her area of operations. Perhaps she had drawn her parameters too rigidly. "Why was his picture in the papers?"

"He used to go to the bus and train stations, picking up teen-age runaways; then seducing them. Raping them, actually, because that's what it is when it comes to a twelve-year old, no matter how willing. And then he'd send them out on the streets."

"Some of the girls at Rundle House couldn't have been much more than twelve when they got pregnant," Susan observed.

"Some of them might have been less than that when he got them started. He was in the papers because an eleven-year-old girl's parents came looking for her. Most of them don't."

"And he's still running around loose?"

"That was a couple of years ago. Maybe he served some time. You know what the law in New York is like. It isn't as if he were a stock manipulator or an inside trader. Or if the girl's parents had been middle class or of the right ethnic persuasion."

"You mean that all the girls in Rundle House are prostitutes?"

"Couldn't you tell just by looking at them?"

"Hard to tell with today's fashions. Streetwalker seems to be the current role model."

"I don't suppose all of the girls are hookers," Jill conceded. "Or even that all of those who are hookers are his girls. But I'm sure most of the gang that followed us are."

Both of them had continued to stare at the man in the Cadillac while they were speaking. He rolled down the window and smiled at them, the smile widening to a leer as he took in Jill from head to toe. He leaned out of the car. "Hey, Momma," he called, "You're a little over the hill for my customers, but I'm the sophisticated type. I could go for you myself. Whaddya say you ditch auntie and let me take you for a ride?"

Jill spat at him. Susan wished she would find some other way of expressing her displeasure. She dragged her away. They walked toward Broadway, followed by the sound of his mocking laughter. "People like that should be killed," Jill said. She stared defiantly at Susan. Susan shrugged.

BROADWAY WAS A relief. It was wide and crowded and cheerful, with bright lights, stores, and street vendors selling books, fruit, and other wholesome things. The beggars—or homeless people, as they were now called—smiled as they asked for money to buy soup and bread and vitamins. Even the garbage seemed neater. There was plenty of noise, street musicians combining with boom boxes and the ever-present workmen tearing up the streets to create a cacophony that seemed to bother no one. Cabs, buses, cars, and the occasional police cruiser went up one side of the avenue and came down the other. Ambulances and fire trucks clanged and shrilled merrily. Susan felt as if she had come back to civilization. She gave generously to the alms-seekers, to Jill's obvious disapproval. Jill did not believe in nondeductible charity.

"Let's not get a cab right away," Jill said. "I need a drink."

"I could use one, too." Actually, Susan felt no particular desire for a drink, but it fitted in with the plan she was beginning to formulate. They went into a restaurant of respectable aspect, sat down at a booth in the bar, and ordered.

"I wonder which building they're planning to buy," Susan said, "the apartment house or the brownstone?"

"The apartment house. They already own the brownstone."

"What makes you think so?"

"Because there was a door in the reception room that didn't seemed to lead anywhere. First I thought it was a fire door, but the fire doors were marked 'Exit,' And it was locked."

"You mean you tried it?"

"How else would I know it was locked? Then I remembered that the brownstone was built smack against Rundle House, so the door would have to go there or lead into an airwell inside the brownstone's property line. So, either way, it's got to belong to them."

"Now that I think of it," Susan said, "there used to be a trustees' room on the ground floor and that space seems to have been turned into offices. And there was an apartment for the director on the top floor, but that's all bedrooms now. Maybe they put the trustees' room next door and Ms. Fischetti has an apartment there."

"I'd hate to live in that neighborhood myself, but it isn't easy to find an affordable apartment in Manhattan these days, even if your godfather is one of the trustees. Maybe that's one of the attractions of the job."

"Salary could be another. The Rundles were always generous with their employees."

The waitress placed glasses before them. Jill drank her bourbon and soda in thirsty gulps. Susan sipped her vodka martini. She wanted nothing to affect the clarity of her thought. Or her actions.

"What's between you and this Berry—Berengaria, God what a name —Rundle, anyway?" Jill asked.

Susan was startled. Whatever had possessed Jill to come up with that question?

"I saw your face when Lucy suggested you all get together."

Susan hadn't realized she'd been so immoderate as to let her emotions show, but Berry Rundle was a special case. "Oh, we just didn't get along. You know how it is with teen-aged girls."

"I thought you got along with everyone, Susan."

"I try to, but sometimes it's difficult." She gave Jill a meaning look.

Jill laughed and patted her client's arm. "Oh, come on, Susan, you know you get along with me better than anyone else."

Susan was not going to allow herself to be baited, There were far more important things on her agenda. She had formulated her plan; now it was time to put it into action. She gave a muffled exclamation and started to rummage in her handbag. "Oh, bother, I must have left my address book over at Rundle House."

Jill looked at her inquiringly.

"Lucy wanted the addresses of some people we both knew. I gave them to her while we were in Ms. Fischetti's office and you were snooping around outside."

"I was not snooping. I never snoop. I was just taking an intelligent interest."

Susan refused to dignify that statement with a reply. "I'm afraid you're no longer *persona grata* there," she said. "In fact, I'm not entirely sure that I am. So I think it might be a good idea if you stay here and have another drink while I run back and get the address book. It shouldn't take more than a few minutes."

21

Jill half rose, then subsided in her seat. "Sure you don't mind? I feel guilty about letting you go back there alone, especially at night."

"I'd rather face the potential dangers of the street than the actual wrath of Ms. Fischetti if I come back bringing you with me. Anyhow, it isn't dark yet."

ACTUALLY IT WAS almost dark by the time she got back to Rundle House; but that was all to the good, as long as the onset of darkness didn't bring out the local wildlife. And, if it did, there was the heft of the gun in her handbag to reassure her, although she would have felt even more confident if it had silver bullets in it. It was that kind of neighborhood.

There seemed to be no one around except the young man in the silver Cadillac. No sign of movement in the alleyways. Even the bundle of rags had vanished from the stoop. Nothing appeared to have changed except that draperies had been drawn across the ground-floor windows of Rundle House. Through the cracks where they did not quite meet, she could see a light in the lobby. Somewhere, not too far away, she heard the thin strains of vaguely Oriental-sounding music. It seemed to come from the brownstone next door, but the windows were all dark.

She rang the bell of Rundle House. After a pause, Ms. Fischetti herself opened the door. She appeared to be alone in the reception room. Lucy must have gone home, unless she was elsewhere on the premises.

Ms. Fischetti did not look pleased to see Susan again. "I'm sorry to disturb you," Susan apologized, "but I felt I had to come back and apologize for Jill. I'm afraid she can be quite outspoken sometimes, but—" Susan could not bring herself to say "she means well"—"but she has many good qualities."

"I'm sure she's a very good manager, at any rate. It was thoughtful of you to come back, but really there was no need . . ."

"And I didn't get a chance to tell you that I'd like to buy a whole table at the benefit. You'll get my check for five thousand dollars in the mail. Unless you'd like me to come in and make it out now."

If this had been any of the charitable institutions Susan was familiar with, she would have been hauled inside and held there, by force if need be, until the check was signed, sealed, and delivered. But by this time Susan had already come to realize that Rundle House was not like any other charitable institution she knew.

Still, Ms. Fischetti did unbend a little. "It's very kind of you, Ms. Melville, but all the secretaries have gone, and it really wouldn't be convenient. If you'd just mail the check, that would be fine."

"Of course," Susan said. "I wouldn't want to cause you any further inconvenience. I'll get the check out first thing in the morning."

SHE WALKED DOWN to the corner in case Ms. Fischetti happened to be watching from the windows; then crossed to the other side of the street and came back, keeping in the shadows of the parked cars, so that it would be difficult for anyone on the Rundle House side to see her.

She paused next to the silver Cadillac. The young man inside rolled down the window and grinned at her. "Hey, auntie, has your girl friend changed her mind and sent you to negotiate?"

She took out her gun and shot him between the eyes. A neat little hole appeared in the middle of his smooth brown forehead. He slumped sidewise. The sound of the shot had seemed very loud, but no one came out from any of the buildings to investigate.

She put the gun in her bag and walked back to Broadway. An old line of verse that she had learned in her childhood, when she and Lucinda Rundle had been at school together, came into her head. "Something attempted, something done, has earned a night's repose."

She had, she felt, earned her night's repose.

IV

WHEN SUSAN GOT back to Broadway, she found Jill hovering anxiously about the entrance to the restaurant. As soon as Susan came into view, she leaped forward and clutched her arm. "I thought you were never coming back. I called home. Andy left a message on the machine. He says I've got to come home right away. Some kind of emergency. He must be hurt! Maybe he's dying!"

No such luck, Susan thought. Although she liked Andy, it was undoubtedly true that life would be much easier for her if he were no longer on the scene. "Was the message in his own voice?" she asked Jill.

Jill gave a grudging nod.

"It doesn't seem likely that he's dying then, does it? And if he were seriously hurt, he'd ask you to come to the hospital, not the apartment."

"But you know how brave Andy is."

Since tactfulness was bred in her bones, Susan refrained from pointing out that if Andrew Mackay had been the sort of man too brave to acknowledge that he felt pain, he would not have left a message for his wife; he would simply have expired heroically on the rug. But Susan did not blame Jill for her anxiety. Andy's line of work justified a certain amount of apprehension. He was engaged in covert operations, working for an agency that, he had assured her, had no connection with the United States Government.

No official connection, perhaps; otherwise he would—or should— have felt obliged to report her peccadillos to the authorities. But his organization certainly seemed to have a working relationship with various branches of the government; she had seen for herself the cooperative terms he was on with the New York City Police Department, reluctant though its cooperation seemed to be.

Although Susan wished Andy reasonably well, all things considered, she was relieved that something had arisen to compel Jill to forsake her and rush to his side. It was obvious to her now that Andy had schemed to "drop in" at the art gallery, so that he could join Jill in persuading Susan to have dinner with them at their apartment. That way he'd have a chance to get Susan alone while Jill was wrestling with the dinner, for Jill fancied herself—erroneously, as far as Susan was concerned—to be a gourmet cook, and, like all true artists, she needed to be alone while she was in the throes of creativity.

JILL HAD BEEN aware that Susan would be available that evening, because she knew that Susan had been scheduled to go with Peter Franklin to a dinner meeting of the Neanderthal Society. Then, the day before, Peter had suddenly announced that he'd decided to go on an expedition to one of the more obscure areas of the Amazon Basin to visit a newly discovered tribe of Indians, saying he couldn't pass up the opportunity to investigate them before they underwent either civilization or extinction, whichever came first.

Susan knew the true reason for his leaving was that he'd become fed up with the noise and confusion of the renovations that were going on at the Melville Foundation building. So off he'd gone, and Susan had not been sorry to see him leave as, like most men, he tended to get cranky when inconvenienced. She couldn't help wondering, however, whether Dr. Katherine Froehlich, his former assistant, who had left the foundation after the unpleasantness there the previous Christmas, was also going to be a member of the expedition, but she would rather die than ask him. Besides, he wouldn't have told her the truth, anyway.

No doubt Jill had mentioned Peter's abrupt departure to Andy, and he had seized the opportunity to attempt to get Susan alone and offer her still another of those "assignments" he was always dangling in front of her. As if I couldn't pick my own kills, Susan thought crossly. "Of course you must go to Andy right away," she told Jill. "After all, one never knows. And don't worry about me. I can find my own way home."

Jill hesitated. Although she loved her husband, she treasured her clients, especially this one. "You're sure? This is a pretty rough neighborhood."

"Come on, Jill. This is Upper Broadway, not Beirut."

So she had seen Jill off in a cab, and, after looking over the wares of a surprisingly well stocked sidewalk bookseller and marveling over the window display of a shop devoted entirely to fearful and wonderful embellishments for the feet, she secured a cab of her own. On her way home, she passed several police cars, sirens shrieking, rushing in the opposite direction. She couldn't help wondering whether they were the result of her own modest effort or whether there were other perpetrators abroad that evening.

When she got home, she was sorry she hadn't lingered longer among the delights of upper Broadway, for, sitting in the lobby of her apartment house, his handsome all-American-boy face aglow with the smiles of one sure of his welcome, sat Andrew Mackay, undying, unwounded, unperturbed. She had known him to be a devious young man, but never had she deemed him capable of so despicable a trick as this—or herself capable of falling for it.

He looked pleased with himself. "I knew the only sure way to detach my loving spouse from your side was to send her off on a false trail. And I did want to have a word with you alone. Sometimes I have the feeling that you're avoiding me."

She would have liked to forbid him the house, at least the apartment, for he was already in the house; but that would have aroused comment among the building personnel, particularly since she could not pretend he was a stranger. He had been her guest too many times before. Lucky that he was as unwilling to attract attention as she was. Otherwise, she was sure, he would have been waiting for her up in her apartment. Little things like locks did not hinder someone in his profession.

* * *

26

THAT WAS ONE of the reasons she had fewer regrets than she might otherwise have had that in a few months (the gods willing) she would be leaving the apartment to take up residence on the top floors of the building that housed the Melville Foundation on its lower stories. For a long time, Jill had been urging Susan either to rent out those floors or to move up there herself. Susan might be well-off now, but not so well-off that she could afford to let such expensive real estate lie fallow. For a long time Susan had resisted, but the old loft building where she did her painting had been sold to a developer. Soon it would be torn down and replaced by high-rise condominiums. There was no longer any place in the neighborhood where she could rent suitable studio space. On the other hand, there was a vacant penthouse at the top of the Melville Building that could easily be converted into a studio.

She finally gave in but without grace. "It's going to mean that I've come this far in life only to find myself living over the shop," she told Jill.

"Think of it as being mistress of your own castle. There's even that cute little balcony on the top you can use to pour boiling oil down on unwelcome visitors. Come on, be practical, Susan."

The more she thought about it, the more Susan began to see the advantages of such a move. It was time she left the apartment which she had fought so hard to keep. Spacious as it had seemed in her poverty-stricken days, it was beginning to cramp her now. It was time to make a break, especially since the type of people who were beginning to buy into the building were not the type of people who would have been welcome in the past. These newcomers were boors who seemed to have no idea of the niceties of civilized behavior. Downstairs there were doormen to protect her from people trying to gain entry to the house, but nobody to protect her from neighbors trying to gain entry to her apartment. They would ring her doorbell attempting to "drop in" on her, making it impossible for her to spend a quiet evening at home, unless she sat there, letting the doorbell ring, pretending she was not at home. She could, of course, afford live-in help to repel evening intruders, but that would mean she would have to sacrifice her privacy in another way.

Worse yet, when Peter was around and not off giving a lecture or attending a seminar or spending the evening at the Foundation catching up on his work, or so he said, he would encourage these intrusions. Dropping in on people without notice or invitation was a characteristic of many primitive peoples, he told her. He was delighted to have the opportunity to study them in their native habitat without the inconvenience of field research. And she was too conscious of the fact that it was she who was paying the bills to reprove him for his lack of consideration. If she bought another apartment in another building, she could still be at the mercy of invading neighbors. Standards were dropping all over the place.

In the Foundation Building she would, as Jill had pointed out, be mistress of her own domain, and Peter could always entertain uninvited guests in his offices—far more suitable for anthropological research, being equipped with tape recorders, devices for measuring the sizes of people's heads, and other appropriate equipment. Moreover it would be far more difficult for Andy to obtain entrance to a building that was her own property, protected by state-of-the-art locks and alarms, with a caretaker in the basement and, if need be, a brace of Dobermans in the foyer.

Unfortunately, such a setup would throw her and Peter together far too much. Even though he would be working on another floor, she would always be conscious of his presence below; and, for all she knew, he might feel the same way about her above.

That was no reason for her to feel trapped. She could—she would—take Jill's advice in yet another respect and buy a house in the country. Jill's idea of a house in the country was a place in the Hamptons. Peter's idea was an igloo—or whatever they lived in—in Patagonia. Susan's was to get something in-between, preferably in another country but one more comfortably situated than Patagonia, where Andy would have neither unofficial authority nor clout. She might not even welcome him as a visitor. Which meant Jill would have to be unwelcome as well. I could live with that, Susan thought. Although she had grown used to Jill by this time, and was even fond of her, in a way, an occasional respite from her constant nagging would not be unwelcome.

V

She was still very angry with Andy. She tried to make him feel guilty. "Poor Jill was so worried about you," she told him as she unlocked the door to her apartment. "She rushed back home to see what was wrong."

"As is only proper in a dutiful and loving wife. Think how happy she will be when she gets there and finds another message from me telling her it was a mistake and all is well."

He followed Susan into her study. How heartless he was, she thought. How well he and Jill deserved each other. Sitting down without invitation, he opened his attaché case, exposing a row of colored knobs and buttons and dials. He pressed a couple of buttons; then he twisted a knob, consulted a dial, and pressed another button.

There was a pretty display of colored lights, followed by a series of beeps. Since she'd seen him do this whenever he came to her apartment and also when he came back to his own apartment, she knew he was testing for listening devices. Someday, she told him, he was going to forget himself and run a security check on the apartment of someone who was unaware of his true activities. "And you're going to find it hard to explain why the deputy director of the National Resource for the Homeless"—for that was his cover post—"should be afraid of eaves-droppers."

"Oh, I don't know. There's a powerful landlord group that would stop at nothing to convert all the residential real estate in New York into cooperatives or condominiums—not to speak of citizens who're afraid we're going to build shelters for the homeless in their neighborhoods—and all of them anxious to know our every move."

He sighed. "If we'd known how much attention we were going to attract, we would have chosen another cover. But it's too late now; we're stuck with the Resource. Pity the mayor had to go and give us a Golden Apple for having done more to provide homes for the homeless in New York City than any other organization. Now everyone's expecting even more from us."

"That's what comes of being superefficient."

He nodded sadly. "How true, how true. We've got to learn how to hold back."

Since the social graces were too inbred in her for her to forego the traditional rites of hospitality, she offered him a drink. "Scotch," he said, "with just a splash of soda. You know how I like it." He lifted his glass in a silent toast. She would have liked to throw her wine in his face, but that would have been descending to his wife's level. That was the trouble with good breeding; it discouraged spontaneity.

The phone rang. "That will be Jill," Andy said. "Don't answer. Let the machine take it."

"But she'll worry about me, if she thinks I haven't gotten home yet."

"Let her worry," Andy said. "Do her good. You can call her back later."

Although she wouldn't have admitted it to him, he was right. It would be difficult to listen to Jill's plaints, knowing that Andy was right there with her. But she resented his behavior, the more so because she knew why he had gone to all this trouble to speak to her alone. He wanted her to kill someone.

Ever since he had discovered her other career, he had been anxious to have her go to work for his agency on a free-lance basis; although why his agency, with all its resources, couldn't take care of such matters itself was a mystery to her. She'd asked him about that the first time he had proposed a candidate for her attentions. "There are certain difficulties for us," he admitted.

"That apply to you and not to me?"

"But you're outside the law," he'd said with a smile to show that he was joking, which was the way they usually conducted these conversations, although she knew he was serious. Dead serious. Ha ha.

What he said was true. She *was* outside the law, and she intended to stay that way. When she'd been a paid hit woman, she'd had no choice except that of refusal. Now that she was independently wealthy, she could pick and choose. She dealt only with those lawbreakers whom the law could not touch, like United Nations personnel who committed crimes for which they could not be prosecuted because of their diplomatic immunity. She was not a policewoman, she kept explaining to Andy; the only time she took the law into her own hands was when there were no other hands to receive it.

And she had her limitations. She lacked the expertise of the trained assassin, who could function with the same efficiency (or inefficiency) in any part of the world. She could not follow a criminal out of the country and confront him on his own turf. Even in Washington she was not at her best. Only last year she had botched her killing of the Romanian *chargé d'affaires*, leaving a bloody mess of which she was thoroughly ashamed outside the Lincoln Memorial. The only reason she had taken him on in the first place was that ever since it had become obvious that there was a serial killer at work gunning down diplomatic malefactors, the diplomatic community in New York had become so well behaved as to qualify for near sainthood.

Perhaps she had placed too many limitations on herself. Wouldn't someone like, say, Carlo (the Bat) Battaglia be an appropriate candidate for her gun? The Bat was said to be the current head of the Puzzone "family," the nation's first family of crime in the opinion of many, although there were other contenders for the title. He had achieved this eminence through killing—or, as he climbed in the hierarchy, having had killed—everyone who stood in his way, including all the Puzzones. He was also said to be behind most of the organized crime in the city—drugs, loan sharking, illegal gambling, white slavery, bribery of public officials, and toxic waste dumping; and, except for a couple of minor episodes early in his career, he had never been convicted of so much as a traffic offense.

She could not fault the police in this regard, for they seemed to be doing their best to get him behind bars. Yet, every time he was brought to trial, which happened at regular intervals, he was acquitted for lack of evidence. Witnesses vanished before they could testify, after which their bodies—sometimes dismembered—would appear in secluded spots in the metropolitan area. Jurors turned mysteriously reluctant to vote for his conviction. Evidence disappeared from the district attorney's office. Once the district attorney himself disappeared from his office.

Surely the Bat was worthy of her gun. But how would she get at him? She was not likely to meet him in her own social circles, nor could she march into Federigo's Fish House in Little Italy and gun him down. She would be too conspicuous there. If only he would frequent places like La Caravelle or the Four Seasons it would be a cinch to kill him.

She did not regret having killed the man outside Rundle House. Certainly he was no loss to the community. But she was not going to make a habit of killing pimps. Pimps were simply not up to her standards.

"Now, WHO IS it you want me to do away with this time?" she asked Andy. "Don't tell me; let me guess. You want me to kill Salman Rushdie on behalf of the Ayatollah Khomeini."

"More likely the Ayatollah Khomeini on behalf of Salman Rushdie —and a lot of other people," Andy said. He looked thoughtful. "No, you'd never be able to get near him."

"I was afraid you were going to suggest that I put on a veil and shoot him through it."

"Speaking of veils, have you ever heard of the Begum of Gandistan?"

"There must be a number of begums in Gandistan."

"But only one who's known outside of Gandistan. You must know who I mean."

She did, indeed, as did everyone who read the newspapers and magazines. For such a retiring lady, the Begum had gotten a lot of press in recent years. She had been the principal wife of the late Sultan of Gandistan, having worked her way to the top through a combination of intrigue and attrition. Over the more than fifty years of his reign, the sultan had had dozens of wives, both simultaneously and sequentially. She was the only one who had lasted. Most of the others had died— some of sudden ailments, some by the executioner's axe. A half-dozen (those with the most powerful connections) had managed to escape through divorce. Three had simply disappeared.

During the final years of his life the sultan apparently became monogamous, with the Begum as his only queen—a sop to Western sensibilities, according to some, an acknowledgment of his failing powers, according to others. Whenever he appeared in public, she was always at his side, mute, veiled, but unmistakably a presence. When he passed away, she was reported to have been at his side. Enemies of the regime claimed she had poisoned him.

Her son, Prince Serwar, was the sultan's only legitimate male heir; for, of the two hundred or more children the sultan was said to have sired, no other male survived. The sons who had been young men when the Begum first made her appearance as a junior member of the harem had died, one after the other, in a succession of hunting accidents. Since then, all other male children had died in infancy. Prince Serwar had plenty of sisters but no brothers. His claim to the throne was undisputed. Perhaps old King Serwar had been genuinely interested in forging ties with the West, for Prince Serwar had been educated at Harvard, the first member of the Gandistani royal family to be educated outside the country. Frogface, as he had been affectionately known at Harvard, had been a popular figure, with a warm interest in sports, the opposite sex, and liberal causes, in that order.

It had been expected that once he ascended the throne things would change. The culture of the opium poppy would be prohibited in Gandistan, along with the manufacture and export of its derivatives. Convicted criminals would not be deprived of bodily parts. There would be no more torture of prisoners and summary executions without trial. Prisons would be brought up to at least subhuman standards. Schools and hospitals would be built. Censorship of the press would be ended. Child labor would be abolished. There would be universal suffrage, guided tours, and indoor plumbing.

So far, none of these things had come to pass. In fact, although this might have been only because expectations were so high, conditions in Gandistan seemed to become even worse than before. Even the carpets —their only export outside of opium—seemed to have deteriorated. And now the begum was at her son's elbow, mute, veiled, omnipresent. Rumor said that she was, as she had been for the past decade or more, the real ruler of Gandistan.

The Begum was . . . how old now? No one knew. Considerably younger than her late husband, for he'd married her some thirty-five years before, when he was in his fifties. He was not likely to have taken unto himself a bride of more than eighteen years old tops, for in Gandistan there was no Western nonsense about children bearing children. A girl of childbearing age was a woman and that was that.

So the Begum would be in her early fifties at most. She was good—or, rather, if rumor was correct, bad—for years to come.

"I KNOW WHOM you mean when you say 'the Begum of Gandistan,'" Susan admitted, "although, strictly speaking, the title of 'begum' is applied to women of rank, rather than royalty."

"I'll bear that in mind," Andy said. "What do you think about taking her on? All expenses paid plus a handsome fee to you or the charity of your choice."

Susan laughed. "You can't seriously expect me to go to Gandistan and kill her?"

"Well, no. There would be logistical difficulties in getting you into the country. Tourists are admitted, but not exactly encouraged. And they're always followed."

"Then why bring her up in the first place?"

"Because I understand that King Serwar is going to be coming to the United States within the next few months in order to establish a chair in Islamic studies at Harvard and get an honorary degree, and you can bet that wherever he goes Mama's going too."

Susan was shocked. "You mean you want me to go up to Cambridge and shoot his mother at the commencement ceremonies?" If it had been Princeton or even Yale, it wouldn't have been so bad, but *Harvard*!

Andy laughed and shook his head. "No, I wouldn't expect you to do that, but he'll be spending time in New York, and he'll probably go to parties and things. He used to be a great party-goer, I hear, though with Mama along I doubt he's going to have much fun."

"Not everyone feels that way about their parents, Andy," Susan said.

She had managed to sting him. "Come on, Susan, you know I love my folks. But I wouldn't invite them to a party unless it was—uh—a very quiet party."

"I know," Susan said coldly. She had been invited to meet his parents at a quiet party. They had seemed to feel she was in some way responsible for Andy's marrying Jill, and they had treated her accordingly. Which was unfair, since Susan had met Andy only because he was investigating Jill and her former shady artistic associates. However, they'd proved to have no connection with drugs, which seemed to be his chief area of concern, and their other peccadilloes were of no concern to him.

Susan had been a little shaken to discover that Hal Courtenay, esteemed director of the American Museum, had at one time been one of those shady associates. It was he who had recommended Jill Turkel to Susan as an agent. "She's an excellent woman of business," he'd told Susan.

And that, at least, had turned out to be true, so, even though Jill had rubbed Susan the wrong way from the start—and occasionally irritated her even now—Susan kept her on as an agent and even allowed her to promote herself to manager. Much could be forgiven someone who, rather than shrinking from verbal confrontations, like Susan, actually seemed to enjoy them. Susan had hoped that falling in love with Andy might mellow Jill, but, although it might have softened her head, it had not softened her heart. As for Andy, nothing, Susan thought, would ever change him.

"JUST FOR THE sake of argument," she asked him now, "how would you expect me to get at the Begum? Even if she does accompany the King, she might not go out in public at all. If she does, she's going to sit or stand behind him, along with several other veiled ladies, the way we saw her on 'Sixty Minutes.' How would I know for sure which one she was? It isn't likely I'd be introduced. It isn't even likely I'd be invited. Even if they have a private all-female party, there'd be no way I could get an invitation."

That wasn't entirely true. Susan felt sure she could get an invitation to any party in New York City, if she set her mind to it. And, in the remote event that she was unable to secure an invitation, she could always crash the party.

But she didn't tell Andy that, because she had no intention of killing the Begum. If Andy's employers wanted the lady dead, he would have to find another agent. "Perhaps you could smuggle one of your men into the harem disguised as a eunuch," she suggested helpfully.

"They don't have them any more." It wasn't clear whether he meant harems or eunuchs. "Anyhow, you're underestimating your abilities. If anyone could assassinate the begum, it would be you. You have special qualifications."

"And what are these special qualifications? Beyond my being a woman?"

"Well, only a woman would be able to find out what she looks like."

"You mean you don't know what she looks like?"

"Not—" he began, then stopped. "No, we don't know," he said.

"That does make it difficult, but surely you have female operatives who could do the job."

"We don't have any female operatives at the moment," he said.

"Well, you do have a problem, don't you?"

She got up to show that the conversation was at an end. He remained in his seat. "You're absolutely right. We should have some female operatives, and I'm going to get started on a training program right away, but that's going to take time. Like most bureaucracies, we move slowly."

He held out his glass for a refill. She ignored it. He got up and refilled it himself.

"Even if I could kill this begum or would kill this begum," Susan said, "I don't see why I should kill her. She hasn't done anything wrong in this country. As far as I know, she hasn't done anything wrong at all."

"Don't you believe anything you read?" Andy asked.

"Very little of it," Susan said.

"Take my word for it. Everything you've read about the Begum of Gandistan is true."

She remained silent.

"How about the people of Gandistan. Wouldn't you want to see them liberated?"

"Of course I would, but I don't see why I should be the one to liberate them. Let them get their own champion, one of their own people. What about the King's sisters? Or, if they're squeamish about knocking off their mother, one of his half-sisters?"

"All of them are in purdah, or so I understand. It's hard to break the habits of a lifetime."

I did, Susan thought, why can't they? But there was no point arguing. It wasn't her problem. She told Andy, as she had told him a number of times before, that she categorically refused to kill whomever he had suggested for her consideration. And he asked her, as he always did, at least to think it over.

"It's useless. I'm not going to change my mind," she said, as she had said all those other times. Those other times she had been right. But this time she was wrong.

VI

After Andy had gone, Susan found herself wondering why his group wanted the Begum done away with. It had been obvious why he had wanted most of the other people whose names he had brought up in the past disposed of, but Susan couldn't see how the Begum, no matter what her shortcomings, posed any threat to the well-being of the United States.

It was true that Gandistan was a drug-producing country. However, it was a very small country. Surely it couldn't grow enough opium poppies to make it merit such particular attention. Besides, what good would it do to remove the Begum? It wasn't likely that she cultivated the poppies or processed them with her own hands. If she died, the business would continue under new management.

Perhaps this had nothing at all to do with drugs. Perhaps somebody in a position of power in Washington simply didn't like the Begum and had given orders that she was to be disposed of. Regrettable, but such things often happened in political circles, she knew. What puzzled her was how anyone in the United States or, indeed, anywhere outside

Gandistan, could have gotten to know a lady who had spent all her adult life behind the veil well enough to have reason to want her killed? It was, as another Oriental potentate had observed, "a puzzlement."

Possibly the Begum's life had not been quite as sequestered as the American public had been led to believe by the mass media. If Susan consulted some more authoritative sources, serious intellectual publications that dealt with the Near East in depth, she might be able to get a handle on the Begum. But she was loath to go to the library and look the lady up. She knew that whenever you consulted a book or a magazine in the library, the very act of filling out a call slip put your choice of reading matter into the computers of the world. She didn't want to go on record as having shown any interest in the Begum, particularly as she was not interested in the Begum, only mildly curious about Andy's interest.

So SHE PUT the Begum out of her mind. She would have liked to put the Rundles out of her mind as well, but she was too conscious of her obligations to Rundle House, especially after she looked at the *Times* the morning after her visit there, and saw, buried in the second section (Metropolitan News) a paragraph to the effect that one Philip Lord, many-times convicted pimp and drug dealer, had been found shot to death in his car on the Upper West Side. It was a very small paragraph. Even the tabloids had little more to say. Pimps and drug dealers were found shot to death in that part of town with such regularity that it barely qualified as news.

No notice was taken of the fact that the killing had taken place across the street from Rundle House. But, then, why should it have occurred to anyone on any of the newspapers to make the connection—or even to be aware of Rundle House's existence? It wasn't as if it had been a well-known institution like Covenant House, where even a run-of-the-mill chain snatching would have gotten headlines.

The murder didn't even rate a mention on the broadcast morning news, but then one would hardly have expected it to, what with all the shootings and stabbings that had taken place that same evening, not to speak of the suspicious fires in Brooklyn and Queens, the dismembered body on the Hutchinson River Parkway and the oil spill in the Kill Van Kull. Then there were the less routine crimes, like the bicycle messenger who sprayed affluent-looking women with purple paint, while yelling, "Down with imperialist whores!" as he whizzed past.

Susan wondered what Lord's girls would do, now that he was no longer there to offer them protection. It would be nice if they would go on to acquire skills that would enable them to earn their livings in a more socially acceptable way, but common sense told her the likelihood was that either they would find a new protector or go on welfare. Or both. However, she couldn't help feeling a little guilty, so she wrote out a check to Rundle House for double the amount she'd originally promised.

And, a couple of days later, as she and Jill were having lunch at Leatherstocking's, she reminded Jill of the check she had promised Rundle House, or, rather, that Susan had promised Rundle House on Jill's behalf. "Don't you think it would be hypocritical of me to contribute money to a cause I don't believe in?" Jill asked.

"As long as I believe in it," Susan said, "that's what counts."

"Yes, boss," Jill said.

"Besides, it's a worthy cause, if that cuts any ice with you."

"Worthy, shmirthy," Jill said. "Did you read the brochure all the way through? Did you notice who was on the board of directors?"

Jill couldn't be referring to any of the Rundles, Susan reasoned, because she would have expected to find Rundles on the board of directors. Probably she had spotted some indicted investment banker or peculating stockbroker. She still didn't seem to realize that these were the stuff of which boards of trustees were made these days. As long as they succeeded in evading conviction or served their sentences, they were socially acceptable, providing they had kept enough of their ill-gotten gains to make them worth cultivating. But Jill had aroused her curiosity and she made a mental note to find the brochure when she got home and see what Jill was talking about.

"A worthy cause doesn't have to have worthy trustees," she told Jill. "Write the check or I'll fire you."

"You're very persuasive," Jill said. She took out her checkbook and wrote a check for a thousand dollars, which she handed to Susan. "Here, you mail it so you can be sure I've sent it."

Susan had been wondering how she could suggest that Jill do just that. Jill was being unusually cooperative. I'm going to have to pay for this later, Susan thought.

"Mind you," Jill said, as she put her checkbook away, "I doubt that they're going to have much success with their gala. They should have had it sooner. People aren't going to these charity affairs the way they used to. Money's beginning to get tight. Besides, too many party-goers are getting mugged on the way home. The crooks read the papers and lurk outside. A lot of people are hiring bodyguards, but then they have to buy tickets for them too. The whole thing gets to be too expensive."

"They could save themselves even more money by just contributing without attending the event. I know I'm not planning to go to the Rundle House Gala. Not that I'm frightened, but I'm obliged to go to too many things already."

Jill laughed. "We've been through this a thousand times. You know as well as I do that if the contributors were willing to do that there wouldn't be any need for these bashes in the first place. People don't want to contribute major sums to charity unless they can get something in return—either have something named after them or wear fancy clothes and get their pictures in the paper, and maybe even have some fun."

"Are you planning to go?" Susan asked.

"I haven't made up my mind yet." But she would go, Susan knew. Jill hated not getting anything she'd paid for, even if it meant she would spend a rotten evening. "Who knows," she'd explained to Susan in connection with the Alopecia Foundation's Masked Ball, "I might get to sell a painting or two. Besides, Andy likes to go to benefits. 'You get to meet a lot of upscale drug abusers that way,' he always says."

THE FACT THAT Jill had allowed herself to be persuaded into writing a check so easily didn't fool Susan into thinking that her manager had mellowed. Jill wanted something out of Susan and she was prepared to make minor (tax deductible) concessions as a basis for what Susan knew were going to be major demands.

A show of Susan's paintings was scheduled to open at the Fothergill Gallery in September, and Jill was determined to make a gaudy international event out of it, with a full-time public relations staff working feverishly to get Susan's name in all the right places—and, inevitably, a few of the wrong ones as well. There would be interviews, press breakfasts, press luncheons, and gala openings (one for insiders, one for outsiders, and, possibly, if the demand was great enough, one for those in-between). Thank the gods, Susan thought, that artists—serious artists, that was—were not in the habit of advertising on TV or she wouldn't have put it past Jill to have a video made. Money—Susan's money—would be spent like water. Although she could afford it, she felt that there were better uses to which it could be put.

Susan knew protest would be futile, but she protested anyway. "All the pictures are already spoken for, so it isn't as if I needed the publicity."

Jill gave her the tolerant smile managers reserve for their clients. "Oh, Susan, Susan, we want to keep your prices up, don't we, especially now that there's this talk of a recession coming. And the way to keep your prices up is to keep your name before the public. Do you think the Sultan of Gandistan would have bought one of your paintings for the royal collection if he hadn't seen your name somewhere?"

"Jill, I've told you before, I resent being marketed as if I—the sultan of what, did you say?"

"Gandistan. I never heard of the place either until this little man wearing a turban turned up waving a checkbook. But what the hell, it's a real country—I looked it up—and the sultan is a genuine ruler and the check is a genuine check. It gives an artist enormous cachet to be bought by royalty, even small-time royalty. We really must invite the sultan to the opening. He could be the guest of honor."

The Sultan of Gandistan had bought one of her pictures! Could this be some ploy of Andy's to arouse her interest? But she couldn't see Andy parting with so hefty a chunk of the taxpayers' money in order to induce her to assassinate the sultan's mother. And why would she want to assassinate the mother of one of her patrons? No, she was looking at the whole thing from the wrong angle. She was a distinguished artist. Why shouldn't the Sultan of Gandistan want to buy one of her pictures to dress up his palace? This was just a coincidence—no more.

"It's time we were going," Jill said, "if we want to check on Iverson before we go to the gallery."

Mr. Iverson was the architect working on the Melville Building and, like most architects, he had to be watched carefully lest he go off on some mad flight of fancy. Jill always insisted on accompanying Susan whenever she went to inspect progress on her building. "You're too soft on the man," she would say. "He'll restore the place to its original condition and have it landmarked before you know it if you don't watch out."

So Susan was surprised when, just as they reached the restaurant door, Jill suddenly said, "Sorry, forgot—matter of life and death—must run. Meet you at the gallery." And, jumping into a cab, she was off, leaving Susan staring after her.

VII

ALL WAS EXPLAINED when, a moment later, Susan saw Dodo Pangborn loom on the horizon. Jill must have spotted her lurking outside the restaurant and taken evasive action. The least she could have done was drag me into the cab with her, Susan thought. She's always telling me one of a manager's duties is to protect her clients, and here she deserts me in my hour of need.

Dodo looked after the departing taxi. "You know, I have a suspicion that she's avoiding me."

The rules of civilized behavior being what they are, Susan gave the deprecating murmur suitable under the circumstances.

"It's guilt that makes her act like that. She knows that if she'd only let you show some of your pictures in my gallery, it wouldn't have had to close down."

Actually, Dodo's gallery had been closed down for showing pornographic exhibits—which takes some doing in New York. Perhaps, if she'd been able to get anything else that would attract the public's interest, she wouldn't have had to resort to the notorious Parenti photo-

42

graphs. On the other hand, nothing she could possibly have exhibited—not even Susan's paintings—could have attracted as much public interest as the Parenti photographs.

"Jill has good contacts. She could help me find work," Dodo went on. "But she won't even let me talk to her. Every time she sees me, she runs away. And don't tell me I'm just imagining it."

I wouldn't dream of it, Susan thought. If I had seen you in good time, I would have run away myself. Everybody ran from poor Dodo these days. Susan had been among the numerous victims of Dodo's next project after the gallery fiasco, but prudence and the fact that her contract with Jill had kept her from making any sizable financial investments without Jill's knowledge had kept her from being taken for very much, so she could afford to forgive, unlike a number of her old schoolmates who were very bitter about their losses. Luckily for Dodo, all of them had agreed not to press charges, not because of old-school solidarity but because they hated to look like fools.

Not that they didn't anyway. "Who but a fool would have taken the idea of a fashion magazine for older women seriously?" Jill had observed, not being aware of Susan's modest investment in the venture.

"Oh, I don't know," Susan had replied. "It seemed—seems like a perfectly feasible idea to me. Of course I don't suppose Dodo knows anything about publishing a magazine."

"Dodo doesn't know anything about anything," Jill said, "except fucking up anything she has anything to do with."

Dodo's opinion of Jill was no higher than Jill's of her. "I don't know what that nice husband of hers sees in her," she concluded, after a highly unflattering sketch of Jill's character, appearance, and abilities. "I'm sure he could've done much better than that vulgar little tramp."

"I didn't know you knew him."

"Oh, well, I introduced myself. Told him I was a friend of yours. He was very sympathetic. He said he was afraid there were no openings at the Resource for the Homeless—I've done a lot of charity work, you know—but he'd keep an eye out in case anything came up. And he bought me lunch." She eyed Susan hopefully.

"How nice of him," Susan said, wondering what had gotten into Andy. "I do wish I could ask you to lunch now, but I've already eaten," she added mentally, kicking herself for sounding apologetic. "We ate early because we—I—had an early appointment . . ."

"Couldn't you put your appointment off for a few minutes and have a cup of coffee with me?" Dodo pleaded. "It's so long since I've had a

43

chance to talk to you, and you've always been one of my very favorite people."

What could you say to something like that? "Stop trying to butter me up, you disgusting little sycophant?" That's what Jill would have said, except that her choice of words would probably have been different. What Susan said was, "But really I'm afraid I'm so late." Weakly.

"Can't you be just a little later? I'm sure whoever it is won't mind waiting, especially when it's you. It's so good to have a chance to talk to an old friend."

"Well, just a quick cup of coffee," Susan said, even more weakly.

M. BUMPPO LOOKED ill-pleased to see Susan return in Dodo's company. "But you have already eaten," he protested, as if the meal had somehow slipped her mind.

"I've come back for another cup of your delicious coffee, while Ms. Pangborn has lunch."

Being French, M. Bumppo had not been trained to conceal his feelings. Horror, shock, and dismay all manifested themselves upon his distinguished countenance. "But there is no more room. Every table is occupied . . . except for those that are reserved," he added, as Dodo started to point out the obvious empties.

Susan appreciated his position. Even though Dodo's meal was going to be paid for, he was reluctant to have her hang about his establishment. It lowered the tone.

"I had hoped you would stretch a point for an old and, I had hoped, valued customer. However, we can go to Le Cirque. They always have a table for me."

He groaned. "Oh, I suppose it is possible to squeeze you in somewhere." And he gave them a table in a dark corner, close to the kitchen.

"He has some nerve putting us here," Dodo said. "Surely you're not going to sit still for it. Why don't we just get up and go to Le Cirque and teach him a lesson?" She looked at Susan hopefully.

"Dodo, I have no time to spend going from restaurant to restaurant."

"Oh, all right. It was for your sake I made the suggestion. It doesn't matter where I sit. He can put me in the kitchen if he likes. I don't care." But M. Bumppo's chef certainly would, Susan thought.

Dodo studied the menu. "I'm glad to see M. Bumppo has given up trying to offer his own versions of early American food. Pity he doesn't give up calling himself Natty Bumppo, too. Of all the ridiculous pretensions!"

Susan had often felt the restaurateur had gone a little overboard in his enthusiasm for James Fenimore Cooper, but she wasn't going to let Dodo Pangborn put him down. "He's done very well with those 'pretensions' of his. Leatherstocking's is one of the most successful restaurants around."

"He has a good PR man. Or woman. I expect, since he's French, it would have to be a man. You know, I was going to open a restaurant, but my backers backed out at the last minute. Something to do with me having been in jail. But that had nothing to do with the restaurant business."

It was true that Dodo's conviction had not been food-related. She had done time for having run a brothel—under the guise of a religious institution, but a brothel all the same. The fact that she had been in prison was not likely to inspire investor confidence, especially since it would stand in the way of her getting a liquor license.

Dodo gave her order to the waiter and returned to Susan. "I see you've taken my advice and touched up your hair. You look so much better. Blondes always fade so fast. Now, if you'd only do something about the way you dress. You can take it from me, understated elegance is passé."

DODO'S FOOD ARRIVED with a speed uncharacteristic of the normal stately pace of M. Bumppo's establishment. Clearly he wanted to get rid of her as fast as he could. So did Susan. But how could she get up and go while Dodo was weeping into her oysters *en croûte* with truffles.

"Somehow, whatever I try, I always get into trouble," she moaned through a full mouth. "I'm jinxed, it's the only explanation. Sure you won't have some wine, Susan?"

"No, thanks," Susan said. "Do you think that perhaps your troubles with the law stem from—have you ever thought of going to a psychiatrist?" She didn't think much of psychiatrists, but she didn't think much of Dodo, either.

Dodo looked offended. "It isn't as if I was the only one who got into trouble with the law. I hear your brother had to leave the country a step ahead of the SEC. Insider trading, wasn't it, or something like that?"

"Alex and Tinsley sold their brokerage and are traveling around the world with their family. Obviously if there had been any question of—er—hanky-panky, the sale couldn't have gone through."

This was accurate in fact if not in spirit. For it was from a spirit that Alex and Tinsley had received the stock market tips that had led to their amassing a fortune—the spirit of Nicolas Fouquet speaking through a psychic, or channeler, as they were called these days. The law, so far, did not classify psychic tips as insider information, so Alex and Tinsley were legally in the clear. However, if they continued to operate their brokerage, they would forever be feeling the hot breath of the SEC on their necks.

Since it would be difficult to conduct business under such conditions and since they didn't need the money, being rich now—not beyond the dreams of avarice for in today's greedy world no one can be—but rich enough so they could live in luxury to the ends of their lives without having to lift a finger except to summon the help, they disposed of the brokerage and set forth on their travels. Since neither Alex nor Tinsley was the type to sit around idly, they were planning to go into some other line of work when they returned. "Probably something to do with the environment," Tinsley had declared, "for or against, depending which one's in by the time we get back."

Dodo looked disappointed. "I'm glad to know everything's all right with them. Amy must miss them a lot."

"I miss them too," Susan said.

She hadn't realized how much she would miss Alex. He was the only person she could talk to, the closest thing she had to a confidant.

But Dodo was not interested in Susan's sufferings, only in her own ends. "I suppose you see a lot of Amy, now that you're part of the family, so to speak. I'm dying to see her again."

"She's so busy with her committees and—and things, she hardly has a chance to see her old friends. I haven't spoken to her in—oh—ages." Amy Patterson was Tinsley's mother and an old schoolmate of Susan and Dodo. She had told Susan she never wanted to see or hear from Dodo Pangborn again. Susan deduced that Amy had been another of Dodo's victims.

"Speaking of old friends," Dodo continued, "do you know whom I heard from the other day? Remember the Rundles? Well, of course you do, your family was always so thick with them. I got a brochure celebrating the hundredth or some such anniversary of Rundle House and inviting me to attend their gala. Who would have thought the old place was still going after all these years?"

"Everybody's been getting their brochures," Susan said. Apparently Lucy had had no need for her as a source of addresses, she seemed to have very good sources of her own. Susan's phone had been ringing with calls from old friends who were similarly surprised to receive brochures from Rundle House after all these years.

"Did you notice the board of trustees? Such strange people on it. And the Rundles—I would've sworn at least half of those listed were dead."

Susan made a mental note to have a look at the brochure. If even Dodo Pangborn thought the board members were strange, then they must be strange, indeed.

"I was surprised to see Berry Rundle on the board. Listed as Berengaria Rundle. Hard to believe she never got married. Now you, I can understand. Oh, I know all about Peter Franklin, but that doesn't count. Still, I would have thought that he would have wanted to marry you now that you're making so much money."

Susan counted to five, which was the most a Melville allowed herself in order to gain control of her temper. "You still keep your maiden name and you've been married," she pointed out. She knew that at least one of Dodo's divorce settlements had been predicated on the stipulation that Dodo cease using her former husband's name.

"With me it's different," Dodo said, shoveling paillard of salmon into her mouth. "I'm a career woman."

"Which career were you referring to?"

"All of them," she said, attacking the crusty rolls.

"As a matter of fact, Lucy Rundle told me Berry was a widow, so she must have been married at least once."

"So you've been in touch with Lucy and not with Berry? That's funny, when you and Berry were so close, even though she was four years older."

"Three. And we weren't really close, while Lucy and I were schoolmates."

"Remember those camping trips your father was always taking the two of you on? You and Berry, I mean."

Susan was filled with an emotion stronger than any she'd felt in years. She kept her voice calm. "Father took me on lots of camping trips, and we often took one or two of my friends along, since Mother didn't care for camping. I believe we even took you once."

Dodo laughed. "That was a disaster, wasn't it? I was never the outdoor type. But Berry Rundle was at home everywhere, inside, outside,

47

and in-between. The world was her bedroom. I've often wondered, Susan, whether your mother was as blind as she made herself out to be."

Susan looked Dodo in the eye. "I haven't the faintest idea what you're talking about."

Dodo wagged an arch finger. "Oh, yes, you do. You can't fool me. Don't tell me it still bothers you after all these years."

"My goodness, I didn't realize how late it was," Susan said, without bothering to look at her watch. She got up. "If I don't leave this instant, I'll miss Mr. Iverson; he's the architect who's working on my place."

"He's the architect who's working on everybody's place this year. Maybe I should have taken up architecture. Interior design, anyway. I always had a flair—"

"Goodbye, Dodo, enjoy your lunch." *And may you choke on your mousse.* "Don't worry, I'll sign for your check on the way out," she said loudly.

But, if Dodo felt humiliated, it didn't show. "Don't forget to send me a ticket to the opening of your show," she called after her departing hostess. "At least that won't cost you anything."

Susan left the restaurant, conscious of the fact that M. Bumppo was giving her back reproachful glances. So let Dodo badger his other customers, Susan thought; into each life some rain must fall. She must watch herself. She was developing antisocial tendencies.

SHE REMEMBERED THOSE camping trips all right. At the beginning she had wondered why Berry Rundle, who was not only older than she was but mature and sophisticated beyond her years, had wanted to go camping with her. All the same, she couldn't help feeling flattered that Berry would want her as a friend. Even when, as time went on, it was only Berry who was asked to join them on their camping trips and none of her other friends, it seemed perfectly natural. Most of the other girls didn't care for guns, didn't even know how to shoot.

Shooting was her father's favorite sport. He had turned Susan into an expert shot. However, she liked to shoot at targets. She did not like to kill innocent animals. He liked to kill animals, regardless of their innocence or guilt.

Berry was also a killer, and also, as Susan recalled, a pretty fair shot. Both she and Susan's father teased Susan for being so "squeamish." She had good-naturedly put up with their teasing, glad she no longer needed to feel guilty about spoiling her father's sport. She kept herself busy by sketching the local wildflowers and taking long walks to observe the beauties of nature. She hadn't realized how much Berry had contributed to her father's sport until, early one morning in the course of one of those long nature walks, she had caught the two of them *in flagrante* in a duck blind.

She should have been suspicious long before, she realized, because she had not been so innocent as to be unaware of Berry's sexual proclivities. The chauffeur, the gardener, the music teacher—that was to be expected. But a father—her father—that went beyond the pale. Even Berry's father—the infamous Edmund—never messed around with his daughter's friends.

There was a scene. Her father blustered. Berry wept. Susan raised her voice.

Later, when her father was off stowing their gear in the station wagon, Berry's tears vanished. "If you breathe a word to anybody—anybody at all—about this, Susan Melville, I'm going to break every bone in your body, bone by bone!"

Remembering what Berry had done to the gym teacher at her last school, Susan knew this was no idle threat. But that wasn't the reason she never told anybody what had happened. It was because she could not bear to think about it.

She never spoke to Berry again. And, by the time both Berry and Berry's father vanished from the scene a couple of years later, she had almost forgotten that episode in her life. It must have been festering away in her subconscious, though, for, now that Dodo had brought it out, she found she felt angrier at Berry than ever.

VIII

SHE DID NOT, after all, go to the Melville Foundation Building to confer with the architect, nor did she go to the Fothergill Gallery to confer with Jill and Freddy Fothergill. She was in no mood for conferences. What she wanted was to go home and brood. She went home, but there was an impediment to her brooding. Michelle, her housekeeper, was there.

Michelle did not attempt to conceal her displeasure at her employer's unexpected appearance. "I thought you was gonna be out for the afternoon. You said you was gonna be out for the afternoon."

"I changed my mind. Please bring me a vodka martini, turn off the television, and try to work as quietly as possible."

"Maybe I should take the rest of the day off. That way I won't bother you in case you got a headache or somethin'."

"I don't have a headache. I feel fine. I just have some paper-work that needs to be done in a hurry," she said, to forestall any conversational attempts.

She went to her study. Presently Michelle came in, bearing a glass on a tray that also held a bottle of aspirin. "Thank you, Michelle," she said. Michelle opened her mouth. "That will be all." Michelle withdrew, tiptoeing ostentatiously.

Susan sipped her drink and tried to focus on the current issue of *Today*, while Michelle rattled and rumbled in the other rooms. She tried to forget about Berengaria Rundle, about all the Rundles. As a result, she found she couldn't think about anything else. She remembered the Rundle House brochure. This was a good time to have a look at it. Where could she have put it? She rummaged around, opening and shutting drawers, finding all sorts of interesting things she had forgotten about.

Michelle stuck her head in the doorway. "You lookin' for somethin'? Maybe I can help you find it."

"No, thank you, Michelle. It's just a brochure, nothing important. I might have thrown it away."

"If you threw more stuff away, I wooden have so much work."

"If you have so much work to do, why aren't you doing it?"

"I was jus' tryin' to be helpful, okay? Some folks jus' don't 'preciate helpfulness."

Michelle left with a sniff. Presently Susan heard the distant—but not distant enough—strains of rap from a radio. She would have liked to let it go, but that would be setting a precedent. It was dangerous to set any kind of precedent with Michelle. Susan tracked her and the radio down to the kitchen. "Would you mind turning that off?"

"You mean you can hear that all the way out there? My, you must have ears like a bat."

A bat! I'm getting hypersensitive, Susan thought. I've got to watch it. She returned to her quest, and finally she found the missing brochure, pushed to the back of a drawer crammed with invitations and announcements for events she had no intention of answering or attending. Most of them should, indeed, have been thrown away.

She looked at it. The first thing that struck her about the Rundle House board of trustees was its length. Set in eight-point type, it occupied a whole page of the brochure. Most of the trustees listed were, as they had always been, members of the Rundle family. To her surprise, Lucy was listed as chairman. It was true that most of the other Rundles on the list were of so advanced an age it wasn't likely they'd be able to function. She remembered that Malvina Rundle had been placed in a home for the mentally disturbed some twenty-five years before, and, although madness did not necessarily disqualify you for membership on the board of trustees of a charitable institution, it was generally held advisable that the chairman should be *compos mentis*. However, since Berengaria and Edmund, Jr. were, according to Lucy, living out of the country, which would make them ineligible to head the board, perhaps it was not so surprising after all that Lucy was chairman.

What was really surprising was the other names, non-Rundle names that she had never seen before on any board of trustees of any organization she knew—names that, at first sight, seemed unfamiliar, like Douglas Chiang, Philip Lord, C. Montague Battaglia, Desmond Schwartzberg, Gianfranco Molinelli, Antonio Savarese . . . At the same time, she knew she had heard—or at least read of—most of those names. In the society pages? No. Not in the financial pages either. Now, where had she seen them?

Philip Lord . . . Wasn't that the name of the pimp she had killed? Of course. Quite a coincidence that a member of the board had exactly the same name as a pimp who was killed across the street. Or was it a coincidence?

Then a name on the list sprang out at her. C. Montague Battaglia. Battaglia was, of course, a common name in New York. The telephone directory was loaded with Battaglias. And the C. did not necessarily stand for Carlo. Lots of other men's names began with "C"—Clarence, Cedric, Chauncey—all names you would expect to find on a board of trustees. Ridiculous to think the Bat could be on the board of Rundle House. On the other hand, if a pimp could be on the board, why not a mobster? At least he would be in the right financial bracket. Nonsense, she told herself, they're both coincidences.

MICHELLE STUCK HER head in the door. "I know you're itchin' to have me go but you're too polite to say so," she announced, "so I figgered I'd leave early, okay? Have a good night, Miss Susan, an' don' worry if I'm a little late tomorrow on account of family troubles."

"I won't worry," Susan said, "but you might have to."

"Are you threatenin' me?"

"Yes."

"Oh. Well, just as long as we know where we're at. See you tomorrow."

If she comes late tomorrow, Susan thought, this time I definitely will fire her. Should fire her. But good help was so hard to find, might as well stick with the old bad, as break in a new one.

She looked at her watch. Time for the early news. She always watched the news on television. It had become a habit. She so often happened upon candidates for her gun on the news or had the opportunity to observe those already chosen—so much better than the still photographs with which she'd been supplied when she was an employee, and which she had to supply for herself after she had gone out on her own.

The news followed the usual pattern. Yet another trial of Carlo Battaglia had ended in a mistrial, the only remaining witness against him having suddenly recanted his testimony after the others had disappeared. Six people had been killed in the past twenty-four hours, one over the daily New York quota, two accidentally, the rest deliberately; one was what the media liked to describe as an "execution-style" murder. All the murders were thought to be "drug-related." A welfare mother in the Bronx had gone berserk and thrown her three infants out of a fifth-floor window. An abortion clinic had been bombed. A church dignitary, after deploring the bombing, had threatened to excommunicate all pro-choice public officials who were of his own faith and to put a curse on those who were not. The bicycle messenger who had been spray painting rich-looking women had been apprehended and claimed it was a political act to protest female liberation. Tonga had fired off a second manned rocket to Mars. The usual routine.

The rest of the hour dealt with nonviolent, hence less newsworthy, events. A number of celebrities had arrived in the city that day, including several entertainment personalities, a pair of royals, and an ex-dictator who was coming to the United States for medical treatment. For a moment, Susan thought of killing him for his past sins, but decided that he wasn't worth the effort. She'd had enough trouble with the ex-dictator of Mazigaziland, though in the end, it had been an act of God and not of hers that had done him in.

Still looking at the screen, she found herself watching a stocky young man in a turban and sunglasses descend from a plane at Kennedy Airport. Something familiar about him, but he must be a notable of some kind or the cameras wouldn't be focusing on him. She must have seen his picture somewhere. He was followed by a group of burly men similarly accoutred in turbans and sunglasses, though moustached rather than bearded. A few paces after them came several shapeless black forms that looked like sinister bundles of laundry; and proved, as the camera closed in, to be veiled women.

53

"Among today's arrivals is Serwar II, Sultan of Gandistan, accompanied by his—er—entourage," the reporter said.

Gandistan, Gandistan, everything seemed to be coming up Gandistan. First Andy had brought up the Begum, then the sultan had bought one of Susan's pictures, and now here he was in the United States. But Andy had told her the sultan was coming to get an honorary degree at Harvard, as the reporter was now informing viewers, so that was no surprise. If it was true that the sultan never went anywhere without his mother, one of the shapeless bundles must be the Begum.

"Who are the ladies with the sultan, Ralph?" the anchorman back in the studio asked.

Ralph admitted that he had no idea who the ladies were. "And I couldn't ask because you know how touchy they are about their women."

The anchorwoman made a face. The anchorman glared at her before she said something that might offend their Muslim viewers. "None of them could be his wife—or wives—because the sultan isn't married," he said.

"Rumor has it," the anchorwoman added, "that he left his heart at Harvard when he was an undergraduate there. He was unable to marry the young lady, because she was not of his faith."

The anchorman bared perfect teeth. "Trust you to find romance everywhere."

"But I feel so sorry for the poor young couple. To think that a thing like that could still happen in this day and age!"

Susan did not feel sorry for the young man. A sultan should have more gumption. As for the young woman, if a quarter of what Susan had heard about the Begum was true, she'd had a narrow escape from acquiring the mother-in-law to end all mothers-in-law.

ANDY PHONED THAT evening. "Did you see who arrived in town today?"

"The Duke and Duchess of York. Gerard Depardieu. The Portuguese ambassador."

"They did, indeed. And also, in case you hadn't noticed, the Sultan of Gandistan. And his mother. I thought perhaps you might have changed your mind and would like to have a pop at the Begum. They're staying at the Waldorf," he added, as if he thought that of itself would tempt her.

"What reason could I possibly have to change my mind?"

"Oh, I don't know. Everything changes—the weather, pace, women's minds. Scratch that," he added hastily, "What I meant was people's minds, without reference to gender."

"Well, I'm still of the same mind. Look, Andy, this joke has been going on long enough. I'm just an artist with a hobby. I'm not a professional assassin."

"Just sleep on it," he said.

That night Susan had a dream. The Sultan of Gandistan stood at the foot of her bed. He was wearing a turban but the sunglasses were gone. His eyes were large and sad and, improbably, blue. He stretched out his hands toward her. "Help me, Miss Melville," he implored. "Help me. I have nowhere else to turn."

"I'm afraid all requests for aid must be directed to my manager, Jill Turkel," she said. She awoke, feeling vaguely guilty.

THE NEXT DAY Jill phoned to apologize for having deserted her client in the face of Dodo Pangborn. "I'm sorry but I just can't abide that woman. You don't know what a pest she is."

"Don't tell me what a pest she is. I've known her since I was a child, while you've only known her since I became your client."

"I'm glad to see you admit responsibility."

"I don't admit any such thing. All I'm saying is that I've suffered longer from her."

"Well, I've suffered more. As if it wasn't enough that she kept trying to get my other clients to exhibit in that gallery of hers, after it was clear she couldn't get you; and that she tried to get me to invest—either your money or my money, I was never sure—in that silly magazine idea of hers"—Susan blushed inwardly—"she actually goes and asks Andy to find her a job at the Resource. Can you imagine such chutzpah? When she knows what I think of her. And he encouraged her, damn him. He even took her to lunch. I can't seem to make him understand that if he keeps on acting like that he'll never get rid of her."

"Maybe he doesn't want to get rid of her."

"Dodo Pangborn! You've got to be kidding. Why, she must be over a hundred years old."

"We went to school together," Susan said coldly. "She's the same age I am."

"Don't be like that, Susan. You know that wasn't what I meant. Are you suggesting that he's cultivating her for professional reasons, that she's mixed up in a drug ring—something like that? I wouldn't put it past her, but then there wouldn't be any reason for him to bother about it. With her on board, whatever it was would be bound to self-destruct."

"I know," Susan said. So, she was sure, did Andy. Maybe whatever it was he was up to with Dodo had nothing to do with her. Maybe he simply was being kind, although surely he could find worthier objects of charity than Dodo.

"Let's eat before we go to the Foundation Building," Jill said. "I can't deal with an architect on an empty stomach."

They breakfasted together at an obscure coffee shop where nobody they knew was likely to run into them, after which they went to the Foundation building, where Jill reduced the architect to a quivering jelly. Susan wondered whether she could get Jill to do something similar to the landlord of the building where she still had her studio. He was giving her trouble.

BEFORE PROCEEDING TO the Fothergill Gallery they stopped at Susan's house to pick up her mail, which was delivered late in the residential sections of the city to keep even the most well-heeled citizens from getting too uppity. There, among the invitations and advertisements and letters from friends—none from Peter, but mail service from the Amazon Basin was very poor—was a square off-white envelope with the Rundle House logo embossed on its flap. Inside was a chilly little thank-you note acknowledging Susan's contribution and stating that her tickets would arrive in due course. It was signed "Diane Fischetti."

"I got one at my office this morning," Jill commented. "You'd think your friend Lucy would have signed the notes herself, since she's the chairman, even if Fischetti is actually running the place. I'll bet they aren't even having the tickets printed until they see what kind of a response they get."

"That would seem like the sensible thing to do."

"I can't see how they could possibly expect to raise enough money from a gala to buy the building. Probably they expect the trustees to kick in with the difference."

"That's what trustees are for, isn't it? Although in this case, I can't see why they bother with the gala at all. Unless it's some kind of money laundering."

Jill hailed a cab. "I see you have taken a look at the board of directors," she said, as they got in. "I showed it to Andy. He said it was interesting."

"Did you ask him whether he thought C. Montague Battaglia could possibly be Carlo Battaglia, the one they call the Bat?" Susan asked hopefully.

"Well, actually, I asked him about Douglas Chiang. There's a Hong Kong art collector of that name, Sir Douglas, if I'm not mistaken, and I wondered if it could be the same man."

"What's so odd about an art collector's being on the Board of Rundle House?"

"Ah, but he's supposed to be a big wheel in one of the Triad Societies. And they deal in drugs, among other things, which is right up his alley. Do you suppose Chinese gangsters and American gangsters pal around with each other? Like Masons or Elks?"

"I have no idea. What did Andy think?"

"I didn't ask him about that. It hadn't occurred to me then."

Susan felt an unladylike desire to beat Jill over the head with her handbag. "Did he think that your Douglas Chiang and the Douglas Chiang on the board could be the same man?"

"He just said that Chiang was a very common Chinese name. Then he asked me if you were going to join the Rundle House board."

"Where on earth did he get that idea?"

"From me. It's perfectly obvious that they're going to try to get you on the board. Over my dead body, remember."

"Don't tempt me. You know I haven't allowed myself to be persuaded to join any other boards. Why should you think they could persuade me to join this one?"

"Oh, they can probably be very persuasive. Make you an offer you can't refuse."

Both of them laughed as they got out of the cab and entered the Fothergill Gallery. Although Susan made the appropriate responses, she wasn't really attending to the colloquy between Jill and Freddy Fothergill. Wouldn't it be wonderful, she was thinking, if C. Montague Battaglia did turn out to be the Bat? Rundle House was far more accessible than Federigo's Fish House—at least as far as she was concerned.

Of course trustees weren't generally kept on the premises of the institutions they served, but they occasionally came there and certainly were open to being lured there. How could she get to meet the trustees without offering herself up as a sacrifice to the board?

Cultivating Lucy seemed to be her best bet. She would call Lucy up and invite her to lunch, express her interest in Rundle House, tell her how much she would like to visit the place again, perhaps offer some volunteer help. No, that might involve her in something she wouldn't be able to get out of gracefully afterward and she always liked to make her exits graceful. Besides, it might give them the impression she actually wanted to be a trustee. The best thing to do, she decided, was simply to have lunch with Lucy and wing it from there.

THE DAYS PASSED, and she still hadn't brought herself to the point of calling Lucy, when Lucy herself called to thank Susan for her contribution and to invite her to a trustees' tea. It was as if the gods had granted Susan's wish in the perverse way that gods have of granting you your heart's desire in such a way as to spoil your enjoyment of it. Susan's mother had dragged her to the Rundle House trustees' teas, and Susan always had nightmares afterward. In fact, she sometimes had nightmares during the teas. Nobody in her age group had ever done anything but suffer through them, except Lucy, she remembered. Lucy had enjoyed them.

"Lucy enjoys pain," she remembered Berry saying.

"So you still have those teas," Susan said. "Keeping up the old traditions."

"Actually, we haven't had the teas for some time. I was really sad about it. But, now that we're undergoing a sort of . . . well . . . renaissance, I suppose, we thought it would be nice to get started again. And our trustees are anxious to meet you. There are some of them who haven't seen you since you were a little girl."

Susan hesitated. She didn't want to go to the tea and meet anyone who had known her when she was a little girl. She was afraid they would pinch her cheek and tell her how much she resembled her mother or her grandmother or, in the case of at least one Rundle still listed as on the board, her great-grandmother. On the other hand, this was the only way she could find out for sure whether or not C. Montague Battaglia was the Bat.

She temporized. "I'm really very busy with my upcoming show. And Jill is even busier, since she's handling the details." After all, if they were going to start having the teas on a regular basis, she could always go to a later one. Cowardly custard, she told herself.

Lucy sounded embarrassed. "We aren't—uh—exactly inviting Miss Turkel. After all, she only bought a pair of tickets. And her mother was

58

never associated with Rundle House the way your mother was—which is why we're so anxious to have you come to our very first new tea. Please say you'll come, Susan."

"Jill's feelings will be hurt. You might not think so to look at her, but she's very sensitive."

"Oh, I can tell," Lucy said, "and I wouldn't for the world want to hurt her feelings. But, to tell you the truth, she does seem to rub Ms. Fischetti the wrong way, and we're very anxious to keep Ms. Fischetti happy."

Ms. Fischetti's godfather must be a very generous contributor to Rundle House, Susan supposed.

"You don't have to tell Miss Turkel about everything you do, do you?"

"She seems to expect it." She had no intention of telling Jill about the tea, in any case, because, if she did decide to go, Jill would insist on accompanying her. The fact that Jill had not been invited, that she would in fact, not be welcome, would cut no ice with her. I'll tell Jill about it afterward, she said to herself. That is, if I do decide to go. But she knew she was going to go.

As she hung up there was a click on the line. It sounded as if someone might be bugging her phone. Andy? He hadn't seemed interested in Rundle House activities. But, if the makeup of the board was what she hoped it might be, there were other law enforcement agencies which might be interested in anybody who had anything to do with that institution. Looks as if I might be getting into something, she thought, and her pulse quickened with anticipation.

IX

"**S** URE THIS IS where you want to go, lady?" the driver asked as the taxi drew up in front of Rundle House. If he thinks the place looks bad now, Susan thought, he should have seen it the way it was the last time I was here. There had been a vast improvement. Although the block still could not be described as clean in the absolute sense of the word, there was no more loose garbage lying about. The road no longer seemed to be in use as a parking lot. In fact, across the street where once the silver Cadillac had stood, there were only three cars, a Mercedes, a Lincoln Continental, and a Rolls Royce, each with a dark-haired young man sitting on the front seat, each with his car radio tuned to a different station.

The boards had been removed from the windows and doors of the apartment house to the right of Rundle House, and scaffolding was being erected around it in what Susan hoped was not an excess of optimism. On the other side of Rundle House, the brownstone showed definite signs of life. The windows on the first floor were unshaded and, between the draperies, she could see the soft glow of silk-shaded lamps and figures moving about. It seemed to her also that she could hear music from inside, although she could not be sure; there was too much noise from the radios in the parked cars. Jill seemed to have been right about the brownstone. It did belong to Rundle House, and that was where the trustees' tea was being held.

She smiled at the cabdriver. So nice of him to be concerned. "Yes, this is where I want to go," she told him.

"Well, it's your funeral, lady."

Someone's funeral, perhaps, she thought, but not mine.

SINCE LUCY HAD said nothing about her coming in via the brownstone, she mounted the steps of Rundle House and rang the bell. It took some little time before the door was opened, by a dark-haired young man who looked more like a gangster than the kind of person you'd expect to see at a trustees' tea. That was wishful thinking, she knew. She wanted gangsters; therefore, she saw gangsters.

Behind him she could see that the lobby was dark and empty. The offices of Rundle House must have closed early today, as, she remembered, they always did on trustees' tea days. The young man made no move to let her inside. He stood there waiting.

"My name is Susan Melville," she told him. "I've come to the trustees' tea."

He frowned. "Are you a trustee?"

"No, I'm a guest. Miss Rundle's guest. Miss Lucinda Rundle," she added, because there would be other female Rundles around, and she wanted to make her provenance clear.

He still seemed undecided.

"Susan!" a voice called, and Lucy appeared in the lobby. She was wearing a calf-length gauzy garment in a mauve print that was the very epitome of a tea gown, but had probably been offered under the category of cocktail dress, since tea gowns were no longer part of the fashion repertory, unless they had sneaked back when Susan wasn't looking. It had ruffles at neck and sleeve, and there was a lavender velvet bow in Lucy's hair. Ms. Fischetti followed, clad in a dark green wool and brocade suit that was obviously a designer original. They must pay their help very well here, Susan thought.

"I'm so happy to see you!" Lucy cried, pushing the young man aside and embracing Susan more warmly than, Susan thought, the renewed relationship justified; but the Rundles had always been an effusive lot. "I was so afraid you might change your mind and not come!"

"Glad you could make it, Ms. Melville," said Ms. Fischetti, with a chilly smile and an even chillier handshake. Clearly, Ms. Fischetti had not wanted Susan to come to the trustees' tea. Even more clearly, she had been overruled. But who had overruled her? Lucy? Not likely.

Despite the two ladies' welcome as testimony to her bona fides, the young man did not seem satisfied. "All guests are supposed to come through next door," he said. "There's a maid to answer the door there. She's wearing one of those uniforms like in the movies and she's got a list of people to let in. Also she's got a metal detector because Mr. Schwartzberg says it's not polite to frisk people coming to a tea."

Susan remembered Desmond Schwartzberg's name. He was one of the trustees of Rundle House; apparently he was their social arbiter as well. She had read or heard something about him, too, recently, but she couldn't remember where or what.

Ms. Fischetti looked at the young man coldly. "I can assure you that Ms. Melville is not only an invited guest but the guest of honor. She does not need to be—ah—frisked."

That shows how much you know, sister, Susan thought, glad to have escaped embarrassment, if nothing more. But what was this about her being the guest of honor? Probably a ploy to put the young man even further in his place.

He looked cowed. Ms. Fischetti turned to Susan. "I must apologize, Ms. Melville, but these days everyone's got to take precautions."

Against outsiders, perhaps, but that didn't explain why they were having their invited guests searched or why, if guests were supposed to arrive at the brownstone, there was a guard at the door of Rundle House. Ms. Fischetti looked as if she knew what was going through Susan's mind, but she offered no further explanation.

Lucy looked penitent. "It's my fault. I forgot to tell you the party was going to be held next door."

"I didn't know the house next door belonged to Rundle House."

"Oh, Rundle House has owned it for years," Ms. Fischetti informed her. "We bought it years ago when real estate around here was going for a song, and it's used for most of our administrative functions. That way we can use the whole of this building for the mothers."

But the director's office was on the ground floor of this building, Susan thought, and she had seen other offices upstairs, when she had been given the grand tour. How many administrative offices did they need? The trustees' room would be next door, of course. Perhaps an apartment for Ms. Fischetti. But that would leave three floors unaccounted for.

"The tea's this way," Lucy said. Slipping her arm though Susan's, she led her toward the door that had been the object of Jill's inquisitiveness on their previous visit. Susan looked back over her shoulder. The young man had moved into the back of the lobby and taken up a post at the foot of the stairs. Under his tight-fitting jacket, she could see the outline of a gun. He was not guarding the door at all; he was guarding the stairs. But against what?

Then she saw the glitter of eyes in the darkness at the top of the stairs and heard the muffled giggles. He must have been posted there to keep the unwed mothers from trying to crash the tea.

Poor things, Susan thought, they never get invited to the Rundle House festivities, not even those being held next door. She hoped they had parties of their own. Baby showers, perhaps. Did unwed teen-aged mothers get to have baby showers? She must ask Ms. Fischetti later. It would give them something to chat about.

THE DOOR OPENED directly into a large room which occupied the whole of the brownstone's main floor except for an anteroom at the front and an archway that led into what appeared to be an annex in the back. The room was furnished in traditional trustee style—paneled wooden walls, solid mahogany furniture, Oriental rugs, portraits of past Rundles glaring down from the walls. None of the modernistic frivolity of the lobby. This was serious decor, meant to impress.

Advancing over the threshold, she felt as if she had stepped back in time. There was the long table covered with a gleaming white cloth and upon it the huge silver urn she remembered so well. The Crown Derby looked like the very same china they used to bring out at every tea, and the muffins, petits fours, finger sandwiches, and other small comestibles piled upon them the same refreshments—at least the same kind of refreshments—they used to serve. A pianist was playing the same old show tunes on what looked like the same old Bechstein. There even was the same smell of furniture polish.

One obvious change had been made. A bar had been set up in one corner, with a white-jacketed barman presiding over it. There had been a bar in the old days, too, but discreetly hidden in an adjoining room, so that old Mrs. Rundle could pretend to be unaware of its existence. "We have to have it; otherwise we'd never get any of the gentlemen to come," Susan could hear the younger Mrs. Rundle whisper to Susan's mother. Not that, even with this inducement, very many of the men put in an appearance at the teas. The atmosphere alone would put a dampener on their spirits, her father had been heard to observe.

Today there were a lot more men present than there had been in the old days. At first sight most of the people there seemed unfamiliar; then she picked out a few aged and bewildered-looking Rundles who had apparently been hauled out of their retreats, dusted off, and propped up here and there among the furniture, holding teacups in their shaky hands and smiling vacantly.

And of course she recognized the chunky, middle-aged man in the custom-made Italian silk suit who was talking to the imposing-looking lady behind the tea urn. He was, as she had come to expect by this time, Carlo Battaglia, C. Montague Battaglia, the Bat himself, the man she had so often seen and hissed in her mind on TV, the man for whose sake she had come here. If she needed further confirmation of his identity, the small weasel-faced man in English tweeds at his elbow was the small weasel-faced man who had been at the Bat's elbow every time she saw him entering or leaving a courtroom, the man who kept smiling at reporters with perfectly capped teeth and saying, "Mr. Battaglia has nothing to say at this time."

Name and face came together. His lawyer. Desmond Schwartzberg. Mouthpiece for the mob. *New York* magazine had done a feature on him. He sounded like a slimebag. He also sounded like the lawyer she'd want to hire if ever she should happen to get caught in her avocational activities. His clients always seemed to get off, although the judge and jury weren't always so lucky.

SHE WAS, OF course, gratified to see the Bat. It meant that she had not inflicted this ghastly fête on herself in vain. At the same time, she found herself even more stirred by the sight of the woman sitting behind the urn, the woman who rose to her feet upon catching sight of Susan and cried, in a stentorian voice that boomed back over the years, "Susan Melville! Long time no see!"

Susan halted in her tracks. "Hello, Berry," she said. "It has been a long time, hasn't it? My, you have grown a lot." Berengaria Rundle seemed to be over six feet tall, but who knew how high the heels might be under the shimmering caftan of heavy green silk that swept the floor, as, abandoning the Bat and his lawyer, she swept across the room and enfolded Susan in an embrace even warmer than her sister's.

Really, Susan thought, if she's going to go around hugging people, she shouldn't douse herself in cheap (though probably pricey) Oriental perfume. Through the thick makeup and the extra chins, Berry was barely recognizable. If only Daddy could see her now, Susan thought, but her father was dead; and, if he had still been alive, probably he wouldn't even have remembered who Berry was.

Berry seemed to have done well for herself financially, either through marriage or other means, for the outsize emeralds and diamonds clustering around her neck and wrists and dripping from her ears were all vulgarly real without a doubt. There was even a diamond fillet threaded through the black braid that crowned her head, creating a tiara effect that was most unsuitable for a tea. Evidently she didn't worry about getting mugged on the way home, Susan thought.

The caftan obscured the lines of Berry's figure, but couldn't hide the fact that she had increased in girth far more than she had in height. Fat, fat, the water rat, Susan thought, regressing.

She looked at Berry and a wave of hatred engulfed her. She didn't want to kill the Bat—yes, she did want to kill the Bat, but even more did she want to kill Berry Rundle. Now, now, she chided herself, a Melville must let herself be controlled by reason, not desire, but she did not feel at all reasonable.

Berry kneaded her arm. "When they told me you were coming to the tea, I was so excited I could hardly wait."

"She was like a little girl," Lucy said, "so full of questions, asking me what you looked like now and what you were doing and whether you ever spoke of her."

She took her sister's other arm and stroked it fondly. Could she really have forgotten the things Berry used to do to her, Susan wondered.

"I suppose you must be wondering why I never got in touch with you all these years," Berry said.

Susan counted to five. "I've lost touch with so many people over the years. And a lot of people have lost touch with me. It's to be expected."

"Life marches on," Lucy observed.

Berry made a small hissing sound between her teeth. She'd always done that when exasperated, Susan recalled. "I've been living abroad ever since my marriage. While my husband was alive, I never could manage to get away to come back home for a visit. He depended on me so much, especially in his last years."

"I'm sorry to hear your husband is dead," Susan said.

"He was a lot older than me, so it wasn't unexpected. He died a couple of years ago, but I've been so busy getting his affairs in order I've only had time for a few flying trips back to the States. I hope you'll forgive me for not looking you up."

"Think nothing of it," Susan said. "I'm surprised you even remember me."

"Oh, I remember you, all right."

"Where were you and your husband living abroad?" Susan asked. Not that she cared, but it seemed a safe topic of conversation.

Apparently Berry had become a little hard of hearing, because she seemed to misunderstand the question. "He died at home, in his sleep. It was very peaceful."

"I'm so glad to hear that," Lucy said. "I hate to hear of anyone suffering."

Her sister gave her a baleful glance.

"What country—?" Susan began.

"But at least I have a son left to console me," Berry went on, as if Susan hadn't spoken. "That makes up for a lot."

For a lot of what, Susan wondered. Could Berry's marriage have been less than idyllic? She hoped so.

"He's a wonderful boy. Everything a mother's heart could desire, except that he hasn't given me any grandchildren."

"That's because he isn't married," Lucy pointed out. She looked guiltily at Ms. Fischetti. "Of course people can have children without being married or there wouldn't be any reason for Rundle House. But not people like us."

"I look forward to meeting your son, Berry," Susan said, looking around to see which of the young thugs present might be Berry's offspring.

Lucy giggled. "Oh, he isn't here. He said he wouldn't come within a mile of the place again after what happened the time he came to look around. I told him the mothers weren't going to be at the tea, but he said he wasn't going to chance it. He—"

"Come, dear," Ms. Fischetti said, taking Lucy's arm, "you'll feel better after you've had some more tea."

"But I feel fine. And I don't want any more tea. I want to see Susan meet Mr. Battaglia again. It's so romantic."

Again? What on earth was Lucy talking about? However, Carlo Battaglia certainly seemed interested in meeting Susan. He was advancing on her, breathing heavily, or perhaps that was the way he always breathed. "Aincha gonna interduce me, Di?" he demanded of Ms. Fischetti. "Ya know I came here specially to meet this lovely lady." And he indicated Susan with a wave of his arm which would have been a pat if she hadn't moved away.

"I was just going to, Uncle Charles," Ms. Fischetti said.

"I thought he was your godfather!"

"He's my uncle," Ms. Fischetti said coldly.

"It's my fault," Lucy said. "I'm always making that same mistake."

Somehow Ms. Fischetti was the last person Susan would have taken for a Mafia princess, but sociology degrees did funny things to people.

Ms. Fischetti turned to her uncle. "I was waiting for Ms. Melville to finish saying hello to—to her old friend before I brought her over to meet you."

"No, I'm the one who oughta be brung over to meet her, ain't that right, Queenie?" And the Bat dug his elbow in Berry's caftan at the approximate point where her ribs should be. Berry did not look amused.

I wonder if everybody calls her Queenie or whether that's just his name for her? And how does she come to know her well enough to call her by a nickname? Had she been the wife of a Mafia—what did they call them?—don, and was that why she had been lying low all these years? It figured.

"Susan Melville, may I present my uncle, Charles Montague Battaglia," Ms. Fischetti said formally.

The Bat bowed low over Susan's hand. She had often wondered why the media referred to him as "the handsome don." Seeing him in the flesh now, she conceded that he had a certain crude animal attractiveness.

"It is a honor and a privilege to meetcha, Miss Melville. I seen your paintings—Di took me to the museem specially—and I reely like 'em, because you can tell what they're about, not like mosta the stuff they call art nowadays."

Desmond Schwartzberg winced and shot a glance at Susan that was supposed to establish a communality of spirit. She pretended not to notice.

"Acksherly I metcha a long time ago. When Johnny del Vecchio married that bubble-headed broad—what was her name? Mimi something."

"Mimi Fitzhorn," Susan said.

"For heaven's sake!" Berry cried. "I never knew Mimi married a—a friend of yours, Carlo."

"He was my second cousin," the Bat said. "It was a terrible tragedy, him being shot down like that. You don't remember me," he said to Susan, "How couldja? I was a skinny kid—and look at me now!"

He gave a hearty laugh. Everyone else gave a wary smile. "But I never forgotcha. I thought ya were the classiest lady I ever seen." He breathed even more heavily. "And ya still are, even classier, if that's possible."

The pianist launched into "Some Enchanted Evening." Ms. Fischetti gave him a dirty look.

This has to be some kind of joke, Susan thought. Mob humor.

"Uncle Charles—" Ms. Fischetti began.

His voice overrode hers. "I can't tell ya what a thrill it is for me to be on the same board of trusties as a classy lady like you. Not that you two aren't classy," he assured Berry and Lucy, "but you're Rundles. People expeckcha to be on the board. But she's no relation, which makes the whole thing a lot classier." He beamed all round.

"Uncle Charles—" Ms. Fischetti began again.

This time it was Susan's voice that overrode hers. "Mr. Battaglia, I'm afraid you're under a misapprehension."

"Call me Carlo, Susie."

"I am not a member of the Rundle House board of trustees."

He looked arch. "Not yet. But a little bird told me ya were gonna join and"—he laughed jovially—"I wooden be surprised if ya were gonna be ast to be chairlady of the big bash, which I understand is quite a honor. They don't ast just anybody to be chairlady of a classy party like this one's gonna be; ya gotta be somebody special. Which ya are."

And now it was Susan whom he dug in the ribs.

X

SUSAN WAS OUTRAGED. The idea! Taking her for granted like that. Even a gangster should know better. Ms. Fischetti certainly did. She looked dismayed. Even Berry looked uncomfortable. Only Lucy seemed unperturbed, smiling away in her own little world.

I've got to be careful, Susan thought. I don't want to provoke a scene with the Bat. He might go off into one of those screaming rages I've heard of. And I might forget myself and shoot him in front of all these people, which would be not only suicidal but gauche.

She picked her words carefully. "Mr. Battaglia—"

"Carlo."

"Carlo, I know it's a great honor to be asked to be chairman of the Rundle House gala, but, if the chairmanship should be offered me—and really I've done nothing to deserve it—I couldn't accept. I haven't the time to serve on a board of trustees, let alone chair a benefit. They're both very great responsibilities, and I take my responsibilities very seriously."

The Bat looked accusingly at his niece. "Ya promised me she was gonna join the board. I want her on the board. And I want her to be chairlady of the gala." He thrust out his lower lip and looked ready to stamp his foot. On someone else it would have been funny.

Desmond Schwartzberg placed a restraining hand on his arm. "Now, now, Mr. Battaglia, you must restrain your enthusiasm. Remember your blood pressure."

"Mr. Battaglia has a tendency to let his enthusiasm for a worthy cause run away with him," he said to Susan. "I'm Desmond Schwartzberg, by the way, Mr. Battaglia's attorney, and also a trustee."

"Mr. Schwartzberg," Susan murmured. They shook hands in an incongruously civilized way.

"Sorry I didn't get a chance to introduce you two before," Ms. Fischetti said, "But things started getting so—so out of hand." She turned to the Bat. "Uncle Charles, didn't we agree that we were only going to talk to Ms. Melville about joining the board, that we were going to tell her how much we'd like to have her as a trustee . . ."

"Yeah, yeah," the Bat muttered, "but—"

"We can't just rush at her the instant she comes in the door and tell her she's going to be a trustee." Ms. Fischetti's tone was admonitory.

Susan held her breath, but apparently the Bat would take this kind of thing from a relative. He smote his forehead. "I guess I just don't understand how things work in society. But what can ya expect from a simple guy in the removal business?"

Susan was startled. She hadn't expected him to be so candid about his activities.

"Furniture removal," Ms. Fischetti elucidated. "Uncle Charles owns a moving and trucking corporation. Battaglia and Sons. You may have heard of them; they have an international reputation."

"Estimates cheerfully given without charge," the Bat added, "also extensive storage facilities, both hot and cold." His mind appeared to be elsewhere. "I got it all figgered out," he announced. "It's like in the old days. A girl would always say no a couple times before she said yes."

"Uncle Charles!"

He flushed, to Susan's amazement. Could gangsters actually blush? It didn't seem right somehow. "What I meantersay is it's the same with askin' a lady to be a trusty. She's got to be coaxed. I like that. I'm an old-fashioned guy. Sorry I jumped the gun, Susie—"

"But the guns are all in the cloakroom," Lucy said. "I saw them there myself. In the old days people never took guns to tea. To weddings sometimes, but—"

"Shut up, Lucy," Berry said, quite as if it were the old days.

"I'm sorry I was maybe too anxious to getcha to say yes right away," the Bat told Susan. "About joinin' the board, I meantersay, but, like Schwartzberg says, it's such a good cause I was sure ya'd wanna support us."

"Of course it's a good cause," Susan said, "That's why I bought two tables for the gala."

"And most generous of you," Ms. Fischetti said. "That's what made us think of you as a possible member of the board."

Susan could hear Jill saying, "I told you so," but no, they'd been planning this long before Susan made her contribution. Lucy's having waylaid her in Leatherstocking's was no accident. I am never going to eat there again, Susan thought. No more fashionable restaurants for me. From now on it's exclusively coffee shops, diners, lunch counters, places where no one could possibly look for me. "But there are so many worthy causes—the homeless, abused children, AIDS—" here the Bat frowned and she changed that to "incurable diseases." "I can't give my time to all of them."

"Nobody's astin' you to. Just this one. This one is special because—"

"Because your mother was on the board of trustees and it was her favorite charity," Berry interrupted. "Because your mother was my mother's best friend. Because . . ." She stopped there, but Susan in her mind could hear the fifteen-year-old Berry saying, "Because, if you don't, I'll break every bone in your body."

"Of course we can't force you to become a trustee," Ms. Fischetti said.

Her uncle gave her a look. "We wooden wanna force you to become a trusty," he said to Susan.

Lucy put her hand on Susan's arm. "All we're asking you to do is think about it. That isn't too much to ask for old times' sake, is it?"

It was a great deal too much to ask, but Susan made the noncommittal noise that serves instead of speech on such social occasions.

It seemed to satisfy Lucy. "Come, have some tea and then we'll circulate and you can meet the other trustees."

"What a good idea!" Ms. Fischetti cried, more enthusiastically than the suggestion seemed to warrant. "Circulate, by all means. That way, Ms. Melville will get some idea of—get some idea."

Miss Melville Rides a Tiger

* * *

TEACUP IN HAND, Susan dutifully circulated with Lucy, glad to get out of the line of fire for the moment. It turned out that only a handful of those present were actual trustees, as listed in the brochure. There were three aged Rundles who smiled vacantly and said of course they remembered her and one who just smiled vacantly. The elegant middle-aged Chinese gentleman who spoke with a British accent told her he was from Hong Kong and how much he admired her paintings and hoped one day to have some in his collection, so he was probably Jill's Douglas Chiang. Not that she'd doubted it once she'd seen the company he was keeping. Nor was she in any doubt about the occupations of the three Italian men who kissed her hand and smiled and appeared to speak little or no English.

Edmund Rundle, Jr.—although she supposed he was no longer a junior now that his father was dead—was not present. "He was sorry he couldn't make it," Lucy said. "There's always so much to do in Peru."

"I understand it's a very busy country," Susan agreed.

"And we'd hoped Cousin Malvina could come, but this turned out to be one of her bad days."

None of the other people present was introduced. "You can meet the volunteers another time," Lucy said.

They didn't look like volunteers; they looked like hoods. Susan had no desire to meet them at any time.

As Susan and Lucy started back toward the tea table, the door to the building next door burst open and the gangsterish-looking young man burst over the threshold, shut the door behind him, and stood with his back to it. His eyes were wild, his clothes in disarray; there were red streaks all over his face and shirt. From behind him came the sound of shrill screams, fists beating on the door, and gunshots.

"It's a raid!" someone cried. Several of the "volunteers" stepped forward, guns in their hands. Apparently they had not been required to pass through the metal detector.

The young man put up his hand. "It's not a raid. It's those girls. They"—he turned red—"I can't say what they tried to do to me, but I'm not gonna go out there again."

The screams were girlish laughter, Susan realized, the red streaks, lipstick. There was a ripple of laughter.

The young man looked sullen. "When I went to work for you, Uncle Carlo, I never expected nuttin' like this."

72

"Now, Nicky," the Bat said, "you meantersay you can't handle a bunch of high-spirited teen-aged girls in the family way?" There were more shots from the lobby. "And you let 'em get your gun too, dincha?" He shook his head sadly.

This time the laughter was louder.

Ms. Fischetti looked grim. "Don't blame Nicky. You don't know those girls. I'll take care of them. Get out of the way, Nicky." Opening the connecting door, she strode through.

Everybody watched her admiringly. "Now there," said Mr. Schwartzberg, "is a very capable woman. You should be proud to have a niece like her."

"I yam, I yam," the Bat said. "As for you, Nicky, I'm ashamed of you. Go clean yourself up. I'll deal with you later."

Nicky paled. Surely, Susan thought, they wouldn't do anything drastic to him. He hadn't been derelict in his duty, merely overwhelmed by *force majeure*. "You're not—" he almost whimpered "—you're not gonna tell Mama?"

"I haven't made up my mind yet," the Bat said. He took Susan's arm.

"Is Nicky Ms. Fischetti's brother?"

"Cousin. Come have some more tea." He guided her back to the table where Berry was presiding over the urn.

"Some fun, eh?" Berry said. "Trustees' teas were never like this in the old days."

She began to pour.

"No more tea for me, thanks," Susan said. "I've had a wonderful time and I hope to see you all again soon. But I must leave now. Pressing engagement."

She would find some way to kill the Bat at a time when he was not surrounded by relatives and henchpersons. Now that she had been formally introduced to him, it should be easier to get at him. Not easy but easier. Maybe she could hint to him that she might be willing to chair the gala if . . . If what? She would think of something. There was no hurry about killing him. There was a hurry about getting out of there. She didn't know how much longer she would be able to keep control of the situation. If she was in control of the situation.

The Bat gave her arm a gentle squeeze. "I know what you're thinkin'."

She gave a guilty start.

"You're wonderin' what somebody like me and them"—he waved a

hand toward the non-Rundle trustees and their associates—"are doin'
here, why we're spendin' so much time and money on this."

Susan hadn't been wondering at all. Rundle House activities were
being used to cover other activities of a nature she could only guess at.
The only thing of which she was sure was that they were nefarious. That
should have been plain to the meanest intelligence.

Apparently it wasn't "I don't see why anyone should wonder," Lucy
said. "It's a splendid cause."

"Right you are, cookie," the Bat agreed. "None splendider." He
turned to Susan. "Ya see, what we all got in common is that we all
believe in life and Rundle House"—he took a breath —"Rundle House
represents the affirmation of life."

Is he joking, Susan wondered. More mob humor? Am I expected to
laugh? Better not.

Lucky she didn't, because the Bat didn't so much as crack a smile as
he went on, "Somebody gotta pertect the lives of the innercent unborn.
It ain't enough to bomb abortion clinics—"

Mr. Schwartzberg coughed.

The Bat paused and chewed his lip. "What I meantersay is we gotta
supply a alternative to those murder mills without bombin' em or even"
—he looked wistful—"settin' 'em on fire. We gotta act positive."

He glanced at the lawyer, who nodded.

"We gotta take care of those poor teen-age girls so they shunt feel
there's nuttin' they can do but kill their own innercent unborn babies."
His voice rose. "If I could only get my hands on those murderin' medi-
cos—"

"Mr. Battaglia, Mr. Battaglia, as you yourself said, we must take a
positive approach," Mr. Schwartzberg interrupted. "And you know you
mustn't let yourself get excited . . ."

"Yeah, yeah, yeah, I know I gotta watch my blood pressure, but I get
so darned emotional when I really care about sumpin. I'm a very emotional guy. Comes of bein' Italian."

He looked at Susan. "You like Italian food, Susie?"

"I'm very fond of it," she said, startled by the sudden transition.

"What kind do you like best?"

"Perhaps we could discuss Italiar cuisine another time, Mr. Battaglia
—Carlo. Right now I really must rush. I've enjoyed meeting you—all of
you—so much, but I do have a dinner engagement."

"With a handsome high-class fellow, I'll bet. I'm jealous," the Bat
declared with a twinkle.

Hard enough for her to accept a gangster who blushed. Now here was a gangster who twinkled. My heavens, she thought, he's flirting with me. It was the last thing she had expected when she had come there to meet him, but then she'd had a number of surprises that evening, and she had a feeling that if she didn't leave right away she was going to have even more. Unpleasant ones, as most surprises are.

"I will forgive you only if you promise to have dinner with me," the Bat went on, "very soon. I'll call you and we'll make the arrangements."

Looks as if I'm going to have access to Federigo's Fish House after all, she thought.

XI

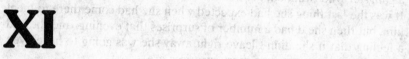

"I WANT TO talk to you," Berry said to Susan.

"We must have lunch together one day," Susan said, starting toward the front of the brownstone, where she assumed the exit must be . . . and the metal detector. She hoped it wasn't retroactive. "Then we can have a nice long talk and catch up on—on things."

"I want to talk to you now." Berry clamped a firm hand on Susan's arm, bringing her to a halt. Berry's rings, great gobs of rock and mineral, bit cruelly into Susan's flesh through the thin material of her sleeve. Susan didn't let herself wince. She would not give Berry the satisfaction.

The Bat beamed at the two ladies, "So nice to see old friends getting together after so many years."

"It warms the heart; it really does," Mr. Schwartzberg agreed.

Ms. Fischetti came back into the room looking disheveled but triumphant. Berry caught her eye. "Let's have some more tea," Ms. Fischetti said, without looking at Susan.

She took her uncle by the arm and led him back to the tea table. Mr.

Schwartzberg and Lucy followed. Lucy settled herself behind the tea urn. "Let's all have lunch together," she called out to Susan.

The Bat looked over his shoulder. "Remember, you and me are gonna have dinner together real soon, Susie. I'll give ya a ring." He didn't ask for her number, which didn't mean anything, of course. If he really meant to call her, he could get it from Lucy.

"I'm so glad you and Carlo hit it off," Berry told Susan, as she urged her, virtually pushed her, toward the archway in the back of the room. "It makes things simpler."

Susan had almost forgotten her original purpose in coming to this place. She recollected it now. Yes, it did make things simpler for her. But what did it do for Berry? Surely she wasn't trying to "fix Susan up" with the Bat? The idea was ridiculous!

"We'll go upstairs where we can be private. I have a little place up here that I've been using—that I'm planning to use as a pied-à-terre when I'm in town," Berry explained. "I expect to be here a lot now."

It seemed an odd place for a Rundle to pick for a pied-à-terre, but one could hardly expect reasonable behavior from Berry Rundle. And why did she "expect to be here a lot now?" Was it simply that having wound up her late husband's affairs she was free to spend more time in her own country? Or did she have some other reason for being "here a lot"—something connected with whatever it was that was going on?

"I've told you I've got to leave now. I have a dinner date." She tried to pull away from Berry, but Berry had a grip of iron. "This won't take more than a few minutes. And it's only a little after six. Even an American wouldn't think of having dinner before eight."

So Berry didn't think of America as her country any more. No loss for America, but what country did she think of as her own then?

Susan tried to protest. "I have to meet my friends for cocktails at seven."

"Nobody ever arrived on time for cocktails in my day, and I'm sure things couldn't have changed that much. Anyhow, there's plenty of time. I won't keep you long, and afterward my driver will take you wherever you want to go, so you won't have to worry about getting a taxi."

"If I can't get a taxi, I can always take a bus."

"A bus! Public transportation! Don't be silly, Susan."

"I could even take the subway!"

"Now I know you're kidding!"

There didn't seem to be much chance of avoiding a tête à tête with

77

Berry. Even if she resisted, she had a feeling that Berry would simply drag her bodily across the room. And no one would blink an eye. The Bat would simply assume that this was the way middle-aged upper-class ladies disported themselves on festive occasions. Ms. Fischetti and Mr. Schwartzberg would pretend not to notice. The others—oh, who knew what foreigners would think?

So Susan allowed Berry to lead her through the archway. Beyond was a narrow flight of stairs, an open door through which came catering noises, and a closed door, which Berry opened. She pushed Susan inside and thrust herself in afterward. The door shut behind them, cutting off all sound from the party.

Susan found herself in a very small elevator, barely large enough for two average-sized people. Although Susan was slim, there was enough of Berry beneath that flowing caftan to make at least two average-sized people. In so confined an area, the scent of Berry's perfume was over-powering. I'm going to be sick, Susan thought; still, if I have to throw up on anyone, I would rather it was on Berry Rundle than anyone else in the world.

But she managed to retain both her dignity and her lunch, and they emerged on the top floor into a small square foyer without any unto-ward incident en route. Ahead of them was a blank wall. On the other two sides patterned silk curtains hung from floor to ceiling. What light there was came from the dim bulbs in two metal wall sconces. Except for the faint strains of a recording playing what sounded like oriental rock, it was quiet.

Berry parted one set of curtains, put her head through, and said something in a language Susan didn't recognize. The music stopped and a woman wearing a plum-colored patterned silk tunic and trousers came out, wrapping a scarf around her head. She bowed to both ladies and held the other set of curtains aside so they could go through. As the curtains closed behind them, Susan heard the sound of the elevator descending.

She and Berry came into a room which seemed almost bright after the murkiness of the foyer, even though it was lit only by fast-fading daylight. The room was good-sized by New York standards, but it seemed small because it was so full of things—Oriental carpets and hangings, silken cushions, ornate screens, carved furniture, gold and ivory and jade figurines, pierced metal lamps, and the like. It was like a room in an expensive Oriental bazaar, rather, an office in an expensive bazaar, for there was a small desk of some wood she could not identify, inlaid with other woods equally unidentifiable by her, all probably rare and expensive. On a carved wooden stand stood a computer, with a paisley shawl thrown over it. Susan wondered whether Berry had decorated the place herself.

There was a reek of sandalwood that Susan soon identified as emanating from a metal bowl on a side table. An incense burner. Susan was sure Berry was not burning incense to conceal the smell of pot, which was what incense burners had been used for in her younger days. She was burning incense because she liked it. Heaven knew what kind of country she had been living in.

I would ask her to open a window, Susan thought, but through the thin gauze curtains and the grille beyond—a common feature of New York windows that led to fire escapes, as this one did—she could see that the room overlooked a rundown, possibly abandoned apartment house, its backyard filled with trash. All that opening the window would achieve would be to add the odor of decaying garbage to the sandalwood.

Berry seated herself behind the desk, and indicated that Susan was to sit in the chair opposite, a carved teakwood affair with clawed feet and ferocious heads on the tips of both backposts. The desk was crowded with a clutter of artifacts, all silk-bound, gold-inlaid, jeweled, and otherwise ornamented to the fullest extent that their various functions would accommodate. Who would ever have believed that the owner of that desk had attended Miss Pinckney's School for Young Ladies, however briefly? Even Dodo Pangborn had better taste, and she had been expelled.

A carved ivory frame held the photograph of a dark, clean-shaven young man in his mid or late twenties, good-looking in a batrachian sort of way. Berry followed the direction of Susan's gaze. "My son," she said, turning the picture so Susan could see it better. "Isn't he handsome?"

"Very handsome," Susan agreed. Where had she seen that face before? Did he resemble one of the senior Rundles? She dismissed the thought. It wasn't a Rundle face. It was a foreign face, an alien face. "Is he staying up here with you?"

"He's here in town, but not here in this building. It's no place for a young man. Or a man of any age. Those mothers! You saw what they tried to do to poor Nicky. Little bitches." But she chuckled all the same.

"I'm surprised you have anything to do with them yourself. As I recall, you were never the altruistic type."

"But I'm grown-up now, Susan," Berry said. "I've changed. There are a lot of things about me that would surprise you."

SUDDENLY SUSAN REMEMBERED where she had seen Berry's son before. A lot of things fell into place. I doubt that there's anything about you, Berry, that could surprise me now, she thought. But she didn't want to disclose her new-found enlightenment. It would not, she felt, be prudent. She kept her face and voice impassive. "I suppose all of us have hidden depths, Berry."

Berry gave her a suspicious look. "Don't try to be enigmatic, Susan. It doesn't suit you."

"I wasn't trying to be enigmatic, Berry. I was just asking you where your son is staying. Of course, if you don't want to tell me—"

"He's staying at a hotel downtown, and I'm staying there with him while he's here, except when I have to be away on business, like now. I hated to leave him even for a few hours, but he wouldn't come up here with me."

"I suppose you can't bear to let him out of your sight."

The intent was ironic, but Berry took her literally, "You can bet I can't. I know he'll go running off to see that girlfriend of his. But how did you know about her? Did Lucy tell you? She's such a blabbermouth."

"Lucy didn't tell me anything. She didn't even tell me you had a son. How old is he?"

"Twenty-eight."

"Surely he's old enough to pick his own friends. And see them whenever and wherever he pleases."

"That's not the way we do it in our country," Berry said. "There, children respect their parents' wishes."

Her son must be a wimp to put up with this, Susan thought. If he does, indeed, put up with it.

"But it isn't just that he goes off like that," Berry said. "He goes off alone. He keeps ditching his—his attendants."

"Attendants! Oh, I'm so sorry. I didn't realize. I remember what used to happen when your cousin Malvina got away from her attendants. And your Uncle Hubert—"

"There's nothing wrong with my son!" Berry snapped. "They're more like bodyguards. It just isn't safe for a foreigner, particularly a young, well-dressed man, to wander about New York alone. Not that, from what I hear, it's safe for anyone to wander about New York alone."

"Things aren't as bad as the media make them out to be," Susan told her. At least the mayhem here wasn't officially sanctioned the way it was in some other countries. But she couldn't tell Berry that until she had told her a lot of other things first. "What's your son's name?"

"I call him Sonny," Berry fitted a cigarette into a long jade holder, the likes of which Susan hadn't seen since her schooldays. "They won't let me smoke anywhere anymore here," she complained. "Some nonsense about it being unhealthy. Unhealthy, tcha! Every time I come back here, they're off on some health kick—fitness, pollution, vegetarianism, no smoking, no drugs, no nuclear power, no nothing. And they call this a free country!"

She puffed furiously. "Do you smoke? The last time I saw you you were too young. Of course, I started smoking when I was eleven, but then, I was always precocious."

"No, I don't smoke. I did smoke for a while when I was in college, but I gave it up. Not for health reasons; I . . . just gave it up."

"Good for you!"

Berry waved a dismissive hand. "Enough of the small talk. Let's get down to business. Susan, we need you on the board of Rundle House."

"It's very flattering of you to ask—"

"I'm not asking, I'm telling." There was an imperious note in her voice, born of years of command, but this was the United States of America, for heaven's sake. Berry had no authority here, no authority whatsoever.

Berry leaned across the desk. "There's a vacancy on the board of trustees and, since you're the one who caused it, you're the one who's going to have to fill it."

XII

THE ROOM DID not go dark around Susan. Instead, it seemed to splinter into a multitude of bright, flickering colors. She felt dizzy, as if she had been sucked into a paisley-patterned whirlpool. She struggled for control. I must not give Berry Rundle the satisfaction of seeing me hyperventilate, she thought.

What seemed to be someone else's voice uttered the words appropriate to the occasion: "I haven't the least idea what you're talking about."

Berry made that hissing sound. "Don't give me that, Susan; you know perfectly well what I'm talking about. I don't know why you shot Phil Lord and, to tell you the truth, I don't care. I always said it was a mistake to put him on the board in the first place."

Susan took an unobtrusive breath. "Am I to understand that you're accusing me of having shot someone named—what was it?—Lord?" She would have laughed, except that she was afraid she would be unable to achieve the correct note of merriment. "Me! You're mad, absolutely mad!"

Berry smiled and shook her head. "I know it sounds crazy, but the fact remains that you did shoot him and you were seen doing it."

"If I had done such a thing—absurd as the idea is—and I had been seen, surely the police would have been called."

"Not necessarily. People around here don't care much for the police, as you might imagine."

"Is that why you live here, Berry?" Susan couldn't help asking.

Berry glared at her. "You want to know why I live up here? All right, I'll tell you. It's because I'm cheap. Don't try to sidetrack me. You killed Phil Lord and you can't get out of it."

"Has it occurred to you that this alleged person who allegedly saw me shoot this alleged other person might be lying through his or her alleged teeth?"

"They wouldn't dare lie to me! Besides, who could make up a story like that?" She laughed uproariously.

Susan counted to five. "Tell me, who was this Mr. Lord and why am I supposed to have killed him? Revenge? Jealousy? Lovers' quarrel?" And she laughed, too, though in a far more decorous manner.

"I already told you; I don't know why you killed him. As far as I know, you never set eyes on him before in your life. He was a drug dealer and a pimp. He was sitting in a car across the street from Rundle House when you came up to him, poked a gun in the window, and shot him. Maybe he said something you didn't like. Maybe you had a fit. Maybe it's your time of life. Some women do strange things when they get to be your age."

I'm three years younger than you are, Susan seethed inwardly. Not that you haven't been doing even stranger things than I have, and starting to do them a lot earlier. But then, as you yourself pointed out, you were always precocious. Aloud she said, "I assure you, your informant, whoever he—or she—may be, is quite mistaken. Unless you're making up the whole thing just to annoy me."

"Now, why would I want to do a thing like that?"

Susan couldn't answer that without getting down to personalities, so she contented herself with a shrug.

"What beats me is how you happened to be carrying a gun in the first place," Berry went on. "I'm told, though, that in New York today lots of people you wouldn't expect to be carrying guns are packing them. In fact, I wouldn't be surprised if it turned out you were carrying one at this moment, since I understand you didn't get to go through the metal detector because Lucy is such a goop."

"What beats me is how a pimp and a drug dealer got to be on the board of trustees of Rundle House."

"I told you I thought it was a lousy idea myself. Beggars can't be choosers, the Fish told me, but I always say choosers don't have to be beggars."

"The Fish? Oh, Ms. Fischetti."

"That's what the girls call her. I understand. And it fits. She is a cold fish. Not the kind of gal you can warm up to."

"She seems very efficient," Susan said, moved by an obscure desire to praise anyone of whom Berry expressed disapproval.

There was a rap on the doorframe. Berry called out what Susan assumed was an invitation to enter. The woman in plum-colored silk came through the curtains carrying a tray on which was a tea set and plates stacked high with what looked like refreshments from the party. In response to a command from Berry, the woman cleared away most of the bric-à-brac from the top of the desk and arranged the contents of the tray on it. Berry spoke to her again. The woman lit several of the lamps—it had grown quite dark outside—and withdrew.

"You didn't get a chance to have much tea," Berry said, "and I could use another cup myself." She poured tea for both. She took milk in hers and lots of sugar. Susan took hers straight. She would have liked lemon but there seemed to be none available.

"Sandwich?" Berry asked. "Tea cake? Muffin?"

"No, thanks, I'll have just tea."

Berry put her cigarette holder down in an onyx ashtray and, after some deliberation, selected a petit four. "As I was saying," she said, through a full mouth, "if you play ball with us, nobody has to know what happened to Phil, except you, me, and, of course, the lamppost."

"And if I refuse to play ball, whom are you and the lamppost threatening to tell? Mr. Battaglia? Or does he know already?"

"Not on your life, and I do mean your life! It would destroy all his illusions, and it's important for men to have illusions. They're not hard-headed and practical like us gals. And I didn't tell the Fish either, in case you're worrying about that, because I wasn't sure how she'd take it. She tends to get stuffy about unauthorized operations." Berry contemplated the plates, took a finger sandwich, and bit into it.

"Then whom are you threatening to tell?"

"Watercress! I told that idiot not to bring any watercress! I hate watercress! Just wait until I get my hands on her!" She caught Susan's eye. "Oh, well, I suppose one couldn't expect her to understand."

She picked up the half-eaten sandwich. For a moment Susan thought she was going to put it back in the plate; instead, she put it in the ashtray. Then she opened sandwich after sandwich until she found something she fancied.

"Oh, I'm not threatening to tell anybody," she went on, through a full mouth, "and the lamppost is out of the country, so he couldn't tell anybody even if he was so inclined. Anyhow, even if he had called the police when it happened, they wouldn't have believed you killed Phil unless they caught you with the smoking gun in your hand. Little Goody Two Shoes; that's what you always were as a kid, and now you're Big Goody Two Shoes."

That was one of the things that had made Susan so successful as an assassin; she was so improbable. At the same time, it would have been embarrassing to have to explain matters to the police. From now on, she must watch these lethal impulses of hers. Any killing she did must be carried out with care and forethought. Mere dislike for someone, she told herself, as she eyed Berry wistfully, was not sufficient cause for eliminating her. Or him.

Berry picked up a cookie. "I just want you to realize I know you're not as pure as you make yourself out to be, and you have no right to turn up your nose at the Rundle House board."

"But I'm not turning up my nose at the board, and I've certainly never made myself out to be pure. I just make it a rule not to belong to boards of trustees. If you don't believe me, just check my bio in *Who's Who.*"

"Oh, believe you me, I have checked your bio. That's what convinced me you'd be perfect for our purposes. One of the things that convinced me, anyway."

Susan didn't ask her what the other things were. She didn't want to know. "I can't understand why you feel you need me. There must be lots of people who'd be glad to serve on your board."

"Nobody with your 'class,' dear," Berry sneered. "And I promised Carlo I was going to get him—us, that is—a classy board of trustees. Sure, the Rundles still have a position in society, but the rest of the board of trustees—well, you've seen 'em."

"It wasn't class that they seemed to lack," Susan said. "What I mean is, Mr. Chiang seemed classy enough for all reasonable purposes to me. And those Italian gentlemen—well, standards in Sicily probably are

85

different from what they are here. No doubt in their own country they rank high on the social scale."

Berry gave her a long, cold look. "What we want to do is bring in other trustees who have class according to local New York standards. We want to make this gala a big success. Your name alone would sell dozens of tickets."

Which was true enough, and one of the reasons Susan didn't join any boards. It wouldn't be fair to the boards she didn't join and would lead to hard feelings among her friends. "I would think that with Mr. Battaglia and his—er—associates on board, you'd be able to get all the money you needed. You wouldn't have to sell tickets at all."

"When did any charity get all the money it needed just from trustees' contributions?"

"It depends on the kind of trustees you have."

Berry took a muffin. "Sure you won't have something, Susan? You didn't eat anything downstairs."

Susan shook her head.

"Well, if you want to starve to death, it's your funeral."

And if you want to eat till you burst, it's yours. For heaven's sake, hadn't the woman ever heard of cholesterol?

"I gather you recognized Carlo even if you didn't remember him from Mimi's wedding. So she was married to Johnny del Vecchio." Berry shook her head. "My, my, who would have believed it!"

"Mimi's been married to a lot of people since then, including a count and a rock singer. Her present husband is a baron."

Berry looked resentful. "My late husband was . . . very well placed, well placed, indeed. You'd be surprised at how high a position he held."

"I'm sure I would." Susan smiled graciously to show Berry that she understood and sympathized with Berry's desire to give the deceased due honor, perhaps more honor than was his due.

Berry picked up her cigarette and puffed furiously at it. "I was hoping Carlo would manage to win his way into your heart before you found out who he was."

"Surely you must have realized that I'd be bound to have recognized him from television."

"I didn't think you'd be a television watcher, or at least that you'd watch any news program but 'MacNeil/Lehrer' and I don't believe Carlo was ever on that though I could be wrong. I watch Cable News Network myself, because that's what we get in my country."

She got up and began to walk up and down the room. As she turned her head to keep her hostess in sight—you wouldn't want to turn your back on Berry Rundle—Susan kept meeting the stare of the animals on the back of her chair, which seemed to have moved slightly in her direction, so that they could keep her under observation. Their eyes were black and white enamel, their protruding tongues blood red, and their teeth very sharp and white.

"It's like this: Carlo has been very generous in his support for Rundle House but he does expect something in return."

"I thought he was committed to the cause of those poor, unwed teen-aged mothers-to-be. Surely the knowledge that he's helping them should be enough; that is, if he's really sincere about his commitment to the sanctity of human life."

"Oh, he is, he is. If he wasn't sincere, would he bomb abortion clinics? No profit out of that. He does it because he believes in it."

"And you—are you committed to the sanctity of human life?"

Berry made an impatient gesture. "I can take it or I can leave it." She sat down again, to Susan's relief; she was getting a crick in her neck.

"What I'm committed to is carrying on the work my family began. Understand?"

Susan was too well-bred to give Berry what in their youth would have been called the raspberry, and perhaps still was.

"Like a lot of people who've made money, Carlo has a yen to make it on the social scene. He knows one way to do it is to get on the board of trustees of a prestigious nonprofit organization. He's even thinking of buying some high-prestige business, like Bloomingdale's, for example. Did you know it was for sale? I was really surprised when I found out. The things that have happened to New York since I last lived here . . . it boggles the imagination." She shook her head sadly. "Altman's and Gimbel's gone, Bloomingdale's bankrupt, Saks Fifth Avenue in the hands of Arabs!"

"I know, I know."

They shared a moment of nostalgic silence.

"What the city needs is a firm hand on the rein, but then the power of the mayor is so limited that even an effective one couldn't do much. Now, if I were running the show, I could clean it up in no time." Berry's eyes shone with administrative fervor. "Let me tell you what needs to be done."

Her ideas were sound, Susan had to admit, but carrying them out would require a total suspension of civil liberties, which would be impractical. Although the individual New Yorker was not unduly respectful of other people's rights, he (or she) set great store by his (or her) own.

Anyhow, the reorganization of the city was not her primary concern at the moment. Did Berry really think Susan was so stupid as to accept the idea of Carlo Battaglia as a social climber, or, even more improbably, of Berry herself a do-gooder?

Apparently she thought Susan was even stupider than that. "Don't get me wrong. It isn't because you're way up in the stratosphere societywise that Carlo wants you. He has a yen for you. He's a widower —natural causes; his wife choked on a fishbone—and he's on the lookout for a new one. I know you'd think a fellow like him would naturally go for some teen-aged bimbo and, all things being equal, he probably would. But he's a family man and he has three grown sons who wouldn't like the idea of him getting hitched to a girl who might produce more sons to compete with them. This way he gets their blessing. More tea?"

"No, thanks."

"Muffin? Sandwich? Tea cake? Brownie?"

Susan shook her head. Almost absent-mindedly, Berry helped herself to one of each. "Mind you, I'm not insisting that you get involved with Carlo, if you really don't want to; all I want from you is that you join the board of trustees. Or trusties, as Carlo would say."

"I still can't understand why Rundle House has come to mean so much to you now, Berry," Susan said, "why it means anything. Lucy, yes, she would do anything for Rundle House, but you never cared about it. In fact, as I remember, you used to spike the trustees' tea with marijuana, long before it became pot, and you sneaked boys into the unwed mothers' rooms until Miss Henderson said, Rundle or no Rundle, she was going to have you committed to a home for delinquent juveniles unless your mother kept you away from Rundle House forever."

Berry smiled reminiscently. "I was quite the little cutup wasn't I? I remember—" she stopped, and the smile left her face. "I was a child then. I'm not a child anymore. I've become aware of my social responsibilities."

"I'm glad to hear it, but please don't try to involve me with either Rundle House or Mr. Battaglia. I have my own responsibilities."

She started to get up.

"Sit down!" Susan stood still. She wasn't going to walk out, because that would necessitate turning her back on Berry. Neither was she going to obey her commands.

Berry assumed a placatory tone. "All right, *please* sit down, Susan. Surely you owe me the courtesy of letting me finish what I have to say."

She didn't owe Berry anything, but an appeal to courtesy could not be denied. She sat down again. The heads on the back of her chair seemed to have grown closer together. Was this one of those trick pieces of furniture you read about in old-fashioned horror stories, the kind that squeezed the unwary sitter's head flat? But what good would a flat-headed Susan do Rundle House?

Berry's eyes were very bright. "What can I offer you to persuade you to become a trustee? Money—I suppose you have enough for your simple needs. Position—you've already got that; it's why we want you. Power? I'm not sure I'd want to give power to you, Susan. So what's left? Your life. You shot one of our trustees. You'll take his place on the board or I'll shoot you."

And she'd enjoy doing it, Susan thought. She hates me just as much as I do her. But why? I have a reason to hate her. But she has no reason to hate me. She's up to her old tricks—trying to scare people into doing what she wants. Trying to scare people for the sake of scaring them. She can't be serious.

"You're joking."

"No, I'm not."

"You wouldn't dare."

"I would, too."

"Somebody might see you."

"It's a chance I have to take. You took it."

"No, I didn't."

"Yes, you did. Don't argue with me, Susan."

"I'll argue with anybody I want to."

True, as Berry had observed, she wasn't a child anymore, and neither was Susan, but no one who overheard the two of them at that moment would have agreed to that.

Susan decided she would have to take the offensive if she was ever to get out of that stifling, overcrowded, claustrophobic room. "What makes you think you could shoot me, especially now that you've warned me? Remember, I'm a crack shot."

Berry laughed. "Sure, you were pretty good at target shooting, but you've never gone after live game. Oh, I'll grant you Phil Lord, but he was a sitting duck."

Was she deliberately, maliciously referring to that long-ago episode at the duck blind? Could even Berry be that crass and insensitive? Yes, she could. She made that clear when she went on, "Even when we were kids you were never as good a shot as I was. Buck himself said so. And I've had a lot of practice since then."

So have I, Susan thought, so have I. And you were never as good a shot as I was. Daddy (Buck, indeed!) told you you were, for reasons which I would rather not think about. I could shoot you right now. Even if you're holding a gun in one of those pudgy overringed hands you're so ostentatiously keeping behind the desk, I could outdraw you. I have been watching too much television, she thought, I might as well ask her to step outside and settle it there.

"You think I'm just talking through my turban? You know how many people I've killed, Susan? Dozens."

You have no idea of how many people I've killed, Susan thought. Hundreds. What a pity she couldn't tell Berry that, wipe that smug look off her face.

"And, now that we're letting down our hair, let me tell you, my husband didn't die a natural death. I killed him."

"But you didn't shoot him. You poisoned him, which takes no skill whatsoever. Any harem girl—" She cut herself short, but it was too late.

XIII

THERE WAS SILENCE. Then Berry's voice came, very softly: "So, you know who I am?"

"You're the Begum of Gandistan, and that's why the Bat—Mr. Battaglia—called you 'Queenie.' You are a queen, in a manner of speaking."

"Not 'in a manner of speaking.' I *am* a queen. I was never a harem girl, and you'd better remember that if you want to go on living."

Susan's hand firmly gripped the gun in her lap. She knew that, although she could kill Berry easily enough, she didn't have a chance of shooting her way out of a building packed with gangsters, thugs, and Heaven knew what other kinds of lowlife. "Yes, Queenie," she said.

Berry glared. Then she laughed. "I keep forgetting I'm not in Gandistan. Actually my proper title is sultana, but I don't use it because it makes me sound like a raisin or something. I don't know why the media insist on calling me 'the Begum'—some kind of putdown, I don't doubt. The foreign press have had a grudge against me ever since—well, never mind that. But you can keep on calling me 'Berry.' No need for formality among old friends."

"Thanks," Susan said.

"Who told you I was the so-called begum? It was supposed to be a secret. If Lucy . . ."

"I keep telling you Lucy didn't tell me anything." Although why Susan should defend Lucy, when Lucy was the one who had gotten her into this, she didn't know. "Nobody told me. I didn't even know you were the Begum or Queen or whatever until you showed me your son's picture. Then I recognized him. Not right away, though, because in the picture he didn't have the beard and the turban—and, of course, the dark glasses."

"What are you babbling about?"

Susan counted to five. "He was wearing them the other day when he arrived at Kennedy. I saw him on TV. I suppose you were there, too, lurking behind one of those black burnooses. You were always fond of fancy dress, Berry, but, really, don't you think—?"

"They're not burnooses, they're *burquas*, and all proper Islamic women in Gandistan wear them to cover their faces."

"So you converted to Islam?"

Berry looked angry. "Of course I converted to Islam. Otherwise the sultan wouldn't have been able to marry me."

A Mohammedan Rundle! Old Mrs. Rundle must be spinning in her grave. But then a Jewish or a Catholic Rundle would have caused a similar revolution, and even a Methodist would have made her coffin rock.

"There ought to be a law against TV. Against all cameras. Nowadays, if you're anybody at all, you can't go anywhere without being followed by them. In this country, I mean. In Gandistan there is a law against them." And she laughed. Clearly it was not safe to be a TV cameraman in Gandistan.

"At least you can hide behind your veil, or whatever you call it."

"And I'm thankful for that. My life wouldn't be worth living if people knew what I looked like."

"Oh, it isn't as bad as all that. I know you've put on weight, but I understand that in some countries plumpness is considered attractive. Just the same, if you keep stuffing yourself with fatty foods like that, you're heading for a coronary."

Berry put the muffin she was about to lift to her mouth back onto the plate. "I meant my life wouldn't be worth living if people could recognize me," she snarled, "and I don't need you to lecture me about my health."

She put another cigarette into her holder, lit it, and puffed furiously.

ANDY HAD EXPECTED Susan to recognize Berry. He had known Berengaria Rundle was the Begum of Gandistan and that Susan had known her as a child so she would be likely to have access to her. But that still didn't explain how he knew Susan would have had reason to dislike Berry.

Dodo Pangborn, of course. No wonder he had wined and dined her; probably put it on his expense account, too. Right then Susan didn't feel any better disposed toward Andy than she did toward Dodo.

"What I don't understand," Berry said, "is how come you paid any attention to Serwar's arrival. With all those British royals and movie actors flocking into the city, I wouldn't have thought you'd even notice the king of a small, obscure country like Gandistan."

"Small, but not obscure. There was a lot about it—and about the royal family—in the media a couple of years ago, just after the sultan died. It all sounded very . . . colorful."

"All lies," Berry said. "Well, maybe not all of it, but highly slanted. I finally had the foreign press thrown out of the country, but that didn't stop them from spreading stories. I thought they'd died down, though."

"They had," Susan said, "but naturally your son's arrival would start things up again."

"I asked him not to come this time, but he said it would look very odd if he didn't come to get his honorary degree after everything had been fixed up—as if there were some kind of trouble in Gandistan— and I couldn't afford any rumors like that right now. Of course he set the whole thing up so he could get to see Audrey." And she muttered something in Gandistani which sounded decidedly uncomplimentary to the absent Audrey.

Susan wondered why a king had to go to the length of establishing a chair of Islamic studies in order to be able to see his girlfriend, but decided, in the interests of peace, not to ask. "The main reason I took an interest in your son was that he bought one of my paintings. Did you know that?"

"Of course I know, you goop. I was the one who bought it. He doesn't know a painting from a poster."

"My manager said something about inviting him to the opening of my show at the Fothergill this fall.'' Might as well put in a word for Jill and her projects.

"He'll be delighted to come, whether he wants to or not, and, what's more, I'll come too—as the Queen of Gandistan, not Berry Rundle. We'll knock 'em all dead with our pomp and circumstance. You just cooperate with us, Susie, and we'll cooperate with you."

Susan was dying to ask whether the Bat was going to come along too, as part of the pomp and circumstance. Again she decided to leave well enough alone.

Berry leaned forward across the desk. "Play your cards right, Susie, and we'll buy a lot more of your pictures."

Susan couldn't help laughing. "Oh, Berry, Berry, did you really think you were doing me a favor by buying one of my pictures? You've made a very good investment. My pictures have been going up in price every year."

Berry blew a cloud of smoke into Susan's face. "Remember this, though. They'll go up even faster after you're dead."

She's threatening me, Susan thought happily. That settles it. I've got to kill her, no way out of it. Self-preservation, the best reason in the world. Then, after I've finished her off, I'll take care of the Bat, if I have the chance. But first things first.

XIV

SUSAN HAD DREADED going back downstairs and out through the trustees' room, smiling and saying good night and shaking hands, as if these had been ordinary guests at an ordinary social occasion. But the big room on the main floor was quiet and empty and, except for a couple of low-wattage lamps, dark. Everyone had gone; the food had vanished; the furniture was back in place. Hard to believe that only a little while before a party had been in full swing. It was as if the play had ended, the set been struck, and the cast dismissed.

She glanced at her watch. Almost eight. She and Berry had been talking for longer than she had realized. Berry seemed to have an almost compulsive need to talk ("You have no idea how good it is to have someone to talk to!"), especially after she'd produced a bottle and a couple of glasses from a locked cabinet. "Afraid it has to be vodka, because a Muslim isn't supposed to touch alcohol, and I wouldn't want any of my people to smell liquor on my breath."

Susan had accepted a glass. She could hardly refuse to join Berry in her toast: "Success to all our ventures." However, she felt sure that she

95

wouldn't want to wish Berry success in any of her ventures, and she felt even more sure that Berry wouldn't wish her success in at least one of hers.

She made only a pretense of sipping her drink, while Berry tossed hers off at a gulp and poured herself another, which she drank as she told Susan the story of her life; how her father had sold her to the Sultan of Gandistan to pay his debts, and how she had suffered as the most junior member of the sultan's harem. "But not a harem girl. I was his wife, which is a totally different job category. After all, I was a Rundle. Dad wouldn't have settled for less than marriage, even if they had applied lighted matches to the soles of his feet, which the sultan was quite prepared to do, until I talked him out of it."

"Didn't it bother your father that you had to convert to Mohammedanism?"

Berry hesitated for a moment. "Oh, that didn't worry him," she said. "It wasn't as if he were a regular church-goer or anything."

"Of course," Susan said, "stupid question."

"I wasn't the sultan's only wife, you understand. He's allowed four at a time, and he already had the full quota, so he had to dispose of one of them so's he could marry me."

Susan opened her mouth.

"Don't ask," Berry said.

Susan didn't.

"She'd been very popular with the other gals, so there was a certain amount of resentment toward me. For years I had to be careful not to eat anything unless somebody else tasted it first. Lost a lot of eunuchs that way."

Apparently she doesn't worry about that anymore, at least not here, Susan thought, or she wouldn't have been pigging out like that. All the same, she was glad she herself hadn't eaten any of the refreshments served to Berry. Unless the tea . . . better not think about that.

"But a Rundle never gives in. I hung on, not that I had much choice, and eventually I got to be senior wife and I could call the shots." Her shoulders shook with mirth. "Little private joke," she explained. Harem humor, Susan thought.

To Susan's surprise, the media had been more accurate than she'd given them credit for. Berry's story was, allowing for a natural difference in viewpoint, much the same as the accounts Susan had read: how, through intimidation, manipulation, and, she admitted, the occasional annihilation, she had achieved that seniority. "But some of those hags were so stubborn there was nothing else I could do. You do understand, don't you, Susan?"

What Susan understood was that Berry was trying to scare her. You, too, could die if you don't do as I say, she was implying. Susan wished she could emit sinister implications in her turn, but both modesty and dignity forbade it. Besides, as she had already pointed out, it was fool-hardy to threaten someone whom you intended to kill and thereby put her on her guard. Berry has made the mistake of underestimating me, she told herself; I must not make the mistake of underestimating her.

She was a bit surprised that Ms. Fischetti had not waited in the trust-ees' room to speed them on their way. After all, even though Lucy was the titular chairman of Rundle House, Berry was clearly the operating head and thus, one would think, entitled to a ceremonial farewell. Per-haps she had waited and given up. Perhaps Berry had indicated that she did not want a farewell committee. Perhaps the niece of Carlo Battaglia waited for no one.

In any case, there didn't seem to be anyone around downstairs except for the swarthy man in a dark business suit and a turban who was standing in the anteroom. He bowed to both ladies; then said something in Gandistani to Berry.

"My car's outside," Berry informed Susan. "I'm going back to the hotel and I'll drop you off on the way. No trouble at all."

As if Susan had been likely to worry about inconveniencing her. But she did not accept right away. Enough that she had let herself be talked into having dinner with Berry and her son on the following night.

She'd been reluctant to accept. She was not anxious to meet a young man whom she expected to make into an orphan. On the other hand, she must not let sentiment interfere with moral imperative. The more she knew about Berry and her habits, the easier it would be to kill her.

Still, she did not like the idea of being penned up in such close quar-ters now with a tipsy, irascible overscented monarch who could not seem to get it through her thick head that her rule was not absolute here.

"No need for you to bother," Susan said. "I'll get a cab. They're not as hard to get up here as you think."

"We've been through all that already. Don't argue with me. I have a car; I'm taking you home; and that's that. And, in case you're worried about me finding out where you live, I already know where you live.

Same old place you used to live in when we were kids, right? Be it never so humble and all that jazz."

"It was our Manhattan pied-à-terre then. My only place now. But it's still considered one of the better parts of the city." Be it never so humble, indeed! Berry might live in a palace, but Gandistan was not generally considered one of the better parts of the world.

ODD THAT BERRY should remember her address after all these years. She didn't remember Berry's ever having visited the apartment. Lucy, yes, but Berry no. Of course, Berry could simply have asked Lucy for Susan's address. Just the same, Susan couldn't help wondering whether, at any time when she and her mother had been staying up at the Pound Ridge house, her father had brought Berry to the apartment. He was a man who liked to take risks, but would even he have dared?

"Why should you think I'd worry about your finding out where I live? I'm sure you wouldn't drop in on me without an invitation." Which was true. Berry might have been guilty of all kinds of crimes, speakable and unspeakable, but even she would not sink that low.

"Oh, I don't know, I thought it might make you nervous for some reason. But how come you're still living in that apartment after all these years? I would have thought you'd have gotten a more up-to-date place, although I suppose you must have had it renovated at some time. Of course you really have to have lived in a seven-hundred-year-old palace to appreciate modern conveniences."

"Surely you have modern conveniences there now?"

"We have indoor plumbing, and there's some talk of air-conditioning once we get a reliable source of electricity, but there's no chance of redoing the whole place. Some kind of sacred tradition. Like landmarking here, you know."

"I'm sure it must be very interesting and historic."

"It's like living in a museum. Matter of fact, once things get going, I think I will turn it into a museum and build myself something on the order of the Taj Mahal. Atlantic City, not Agra," she explained. "That Donald Trump knows how to do things right."

She didn't explain what the things that were supposed to get going were.

"You don't have to feel too sorry for me, though. I do have a summer place up in the hills which is quite comfortable. You must come there for a visit; I promise to give you a good time. Not all of the young men are eunuchs. In fact, none of 'em are, now Sonny's abolished the harem. Where's your summer place, Susan? Newport? Or have you fallen back on the Hamptons?"

"I don't have a summer place at the moment, but I'm looking around," Susan said, trying not to sound defensive. "As a matter of fact, I'm going to leave my apartment soon. I bought a building further downtown a few years ago, and I'm having the upper floors converted into an apartment,"

"Oh, yes, that foundation of yours for scatological research or some such."

"Anthropological research."

"Whatever it is that boyfriend of yours is supposed to do."

"You seem very well-informed about my private affairs," Susan said coldly.

"Well, you're a celebrity in your own small way. Celebrities aren't allowed to have private lives. Especially in this country. And now that you've brought the subject up, I must tell you that Carlo doesn't know about your boyfriend—he doesn't read much—so you'd better not mention it. He's an old-fashioned guy. He wouldn't like it."

"Mr. Battaglia's approval does not concern me. And I wouldn't dream of discussing my private affairs with him."

"Good enough," Berry said.

Susan could have killed her. But I *am* going to kill her, she reminded herself, so I mustn't let her get under my skin.

BERRY BEGAN TO swathe herself in the black garment in which Susan had seen her arrive at Kennedy—or one very similar. "I wear my burqua when I go into the hotel officially, so no one knows what the Queen of Gandistan looks like," she explained. "Then, if I want to go shopping, I just put on regular clothes and take a back elevator. I come out in the lobby as plain old Berry Rundle, and no one gives me a second glance. The doorman calls me a taxi and I go wherever I want. I come back the same way, and no one's the wiser. I've even kept my charge accounts in my maiden name so I can shop in peace."

Susan repressed a smile. The Waldorf was accustomed to potentates and their peculiarities. She'd bet every member of the staff was familiar with the begum's face. Otherwise, she might be able to leave the hotel unobserved, but she'd never make it back to her suite unchallenged.

"But what do you do about bodyguards, then?"

"Bodyguards! Don't be a simp, Susan. How unobtrusive would I be if I went out with a flock of bodyguards baying at my heels?"

"If you're afraid of letting your son go out without bodyguards, how come you're not afraid of going out without them yourself?"

"For Pete's sake, Susan, what's there to be afraid of on Fifth Avenue or Madison or even Lexington?"

She hasn't been reading the papers, Susan thought. Otherwise she would realize that nowadays Fifth Avenue and Madison and even Lexington were hardly the safe havens she fancied them to be. Or that plenty of people with no other distinction than their wealth went around with bodyguards these days.

"I did have a rather unnerving experience when I was here last year —very briefly—doing a spot of shopping incognito," Berry confided. "As I was coming out of Saks, a photographer took my picture, just like that, without asking permission. My first impulse was to smash his camera, but I was afraid that would make me too conspicuous. So all I did was give him a good smack on the head with my handbag, and he ran away."

If she had hit him with anything like the large crocodile bag she was carrying at the moment, Susan thought, she had probably given the man a concussion.

"I figured he couldn't possibly know who I was. He must just be one of those pests who take your picture in the street and then hand you a little card telling you where you send money so you can buy a copy. Still, I was a little surprised to see one of them working Fifth Avenue."

"Fifth Avenue has degenerated," Susan agreed, "but not that much."

"Then, a week or so later, I happened to be looking at the Sunday *Times*—they get it up at Rundle House—and, you'll never believe it, there was my picture. *My* picture! On the woman's page—woman's pages, rather, because they go on and on."

"The *Times* doesn't have a woman's page—or pages—any more. They call it 'Style' now."

"I don't care what they call it; it's the same old guff. This was in a piece called 'On the Street'—'On the Street,' can you beat that? As if I were a hooker or something. There wasn't just a picture of me but of half a dozen other well-dressed, good-looking nonanorexic women. The subhead was 'Queen-Sized Chic.' Oh my God, I thought: My cover's blown. The *Times* knows who I am. I'll never be able to go out without my veil any more. Then I read the article. Guess what it was about."

Susan tried not to smile. "I'm afraid I have a pretty good idea."

"By 'queen-sized' they meant fat. *Fat*! Can you imagine! I got so mad I wanted to sue the paper—start a class action on behalf of female rulers everywhere. But the Fish talked me out of it. 'Your picture got in the paper,' she said, 'which was unfortunate. Still, nobody knows who the woman in the picture is. If you sue, you'll have to come out in the open. If you want to stay anonymous, you have to keep quiet.' "

"Sensible woman," Susan said, a little regretfully. She would have enjoyed seeing the media coverage of the lawsuit.

"What's become of this constitutional right to privacy I hear so much about, not to speak of human rights, if anybody can just walk up to you and take your picture and print it anywhere?"

There might be an answer to that, but Susan couldn't think of one.

THE TURBANED MAN opened the front door of the brownstone. The street outside was empty of cars now, except for the silver stretch limousine waiting in front. The lower floor of Rundle House was dark, but upstairs she could see lights and hear the sound of music (if you could call it music) and girlish voices. The mothers seemed to be having a good time. Perhaps they were feasting off the leftovers from the party, if there were any leftovers after Berry's predations.

The man opened the door to the car. Berry went inside, tripping over the skirts of her burqua. The man continued to hold the door open. After a considered pause, Susan followed Berry inside. The man closed the door and got into the front of the car, next to another turbaned man seated at the wheel. My, we are traveling in style, Susan thought, but she's the Begum now, not plain old Berry Rundle; no need to be unobtrusive.

Berry gave what Susan assumed to be her address to the driver. At least she said something in Gandistani to him. It could have been, "Wrap her in the spare burqua and throw her in the river."

"Where is this Foundation Building of yours, anyway?" Berry asked. "You said it was further downtown than your apartment. How much further? Not down in that grungy old manufacturing district they tell me's become so fashionable—what do they call it?—So What? What Ho?"

"Soho. No, it's uptown."

"You don't mean to tell me that you own that creepy old building your studio's in?"

She seems to know a lot about me, Susan thought uneasily; she must

101

really have been investigating me. But not too thoroughly, or she wouldn't have dismissed my killing of that man outside Rundle House as an aberration.

"No, the Foundation Building's in the East Seventies and it's between Fifth and Madison."

"Now that used to be a really great address, unless things have changed even more than I imagined."

"It's still quite good," Susan acknowledged. "I'm planning to have my studio in the building, too."

"That will be nice and convenient." The burqua billowed impatiently. "God, I wish I could smoke behind this thing, but I've already set myself on fire three times."

There was a glugging sound behind the burqua. Good heavens, Susan thought, she's got the vodka bottle in there. How come she hadn't noticed Berry's putting the bottle in her bag? Maybe she hadn't. Maybe there had been a bottle in the bag already. One thing about the Begum of Gandistan the press hadn't caught on to. She was a lush.

"To tell the truth, I'd like to have myself a place in a better part of town. I lied to you when I said I was staying up there because I'm cheap, but you knew that. I stay there because up in that neighborhood nobody asks questions."

Another glugging sound. "Nobody knows who comes in or goes out up there, and nobody cares. Nobody cares about me at all, not even Sonny."

There was a snuffling sound behind the black veil.

A response was obviously expected. Susan was damned if she would say she cared, even in the interests of hypocrisy. "Lucy cares."

"Goosey Lucy; that's what I always used to call her, and it still fits. I suspect her of being the one who got me a subscription to *Big Beautiful Woman* anonymously."

"No doubt she meant well."

"Lucy always means well. That's her trouble. Anyhow, I was telling you why I keep that apartment in Rundle House. Security reasons. Uneasy lies the head that wears a crown and so forth."

"I thought that applied to ruling monarchs, not dowager queens."

Berry sat bolt upright. Susan could sense her glare, even through the veil. "You will not call me a dowager queen, if you know what's good for you. I'm in charge."

"I thought your son was in charge. He's the king. Yours is only a courtesy title. That's what I read, anyway."

"He's king in name only. He isn't fit to rule. He doesn't have the necessary killer instinct. In fact, though I hate to say this about my own son, Serwar is a wimp."

Here again the media seemed to have been right. The Begum was, indeed, the power behind the throne, and not very far behind, either, judging from the way she was acting.

But why had her son allowed her to usurp his power? Was young Serwar mentally disturbed, after all? He had, it was true, obtained a degree—two degrees, if she remembered correctly—from Harvard, but that didn't prove anything.

XV

BERRY PATTED SUSAN'S knee. Susan pulled away before she could stop herself. "Oh, come on, Susie, you haven't been taking me seriously, have you? I'm a great little kidder, as Carlo would tell you."

Yes, and Carlo was a great little kidder himself. Wrap you up in cement and drop you in the East River for a laugh. Mob humor. Though he wouldn't do that to me, Susan thought. You don't drop someone with class in cement, especially someone for whom you're supposed to have cherished a secret admiration over the years.

Could it possibly be true that he was interested in her as a woman? No, a gangster wasn't likely to have such good taste. It had to be part of their scheme to lure her onto the Rundle House board, though it wasn't clear whether they thought that the idea of Carlo Battaglia's devotion would attract her or frighten her.

But why were they going to all this trouble to get her on the board in the first place? No use asking Berry; she wasn't likely to get an honest answer from her.

Susan picked her words carefully. "I knew you must be—well—exaggerating when you said you'd killed dozens of people. After all, people like us—the Rundles, the Melvilles—don't go around doing things like that, do they?"

"No, we don't. At least not very often," Berry chuckled.

Susan chuckled, too, but inwardly. "But you do come on so—so strong."

"Comes of having been a queen all these years. I can't help throwing my weight around . . . And no cracks," she added sternly. "I'm comfortable with the way I look."

"I wouldn't dream of making any cracks," Susan said. "And what does it matter what you look like as long as you're healthy?"

There was silence behind the burqua. "I'm like the Queen of Hearts, you know," Berry finally said. "I never really killed nobody. For the most part, anyhow. My husband, of course, but that was really a mercy killing. I'd been poisoning him slowly so he wouldn't even think of getting rid of me now that I was getting on a bit, so he could bump up the wives next in line and marry some young chick. I finally decided to put the old goat out of his misery."

"That was very thoughtful of you. And those dozens of people you were telling me about whom you said you'd killed? Before you changed your mind about that."

"Haven't you been paying attention? I said I was just putting you on. Trying to get a rise out of you. Sure, the other wives died, but they killed each other. Or the harem girls killed them, hoping to be promoted. Common practice behind the veil. Besides, they used to torture the younger girls a lot. Really sickening. You must have read about it in those supermarket tabloids that seem to have sprung up all over the place."

"I don't read supermarket tabloids."

"No, I don't suppose you would. Or admit to it, if you did. You were always such a snot, even when you were a kid, and people don't change that much."

In some cases they don't change at all, Susan thought. And I never read supermarket tabloids. I even try not to look at the headlines at the checkout counter.

"Maybe they do go overboard now and then, but there's a lot more truth in them than in the establishment papers, and they're a lot peppier."

Susan wondered whether Berry subscribed to the supermarket tabloids or just caught them on her trips to the United States; and, if so, whether she actually went shopping in supermarkets herself. Oh, if only she did. A supermarket would be such a splendid place to assassinate someone. The body could lie in the aisle for hours and people would just walk around it. Only when someone tripped over it and threatened to sue would the store manager finally deign to take notice.

"Now, what were we talking about? Oh, yes, the death rate in Gandistan. Naturally it's high. Primitive country—poor sanitation, rampant witchcraft, no industrial safety regulations—what can you expect?"

"I didn't know Gandistan had any industry."

"Cottage industry, mostly. But we're going to change all that. Yes, siree, things are going to be a lot different from now on." There was a glugging sound behind the burqua. She'll be lucky if she gets across the Waldorf lobby without falling flat on her face, Susan thought.

Berry's voice grew loud. "Oh, sure, there's the occasional execution. Every well-regulated country has executions. Criminals and people with the wrong politics are beheaded or garrotted from time to time. Publicly. No theater in Gandistan to speak of, and we discourage the importation of movies, so we've got to give the people some kind of entertainment. Then, of course, there are always a lot of accidents—highway, hunting, horseplay—you name it."

She gave a royal hiccup. "Why do you keep looking over your shoulder like that, Susan? It makes me nervous."

"Maybe it's my imagination, but there seems to be a car—or cars—following us."

"It's not your imagination. Cars follow me all the time. Don't worry about it."

She offered no further explanation. Maybe it was her own people in the light gray Dodge sedan that Susan had noticed behind them and the dark green Mercury hatchback that seemed to be following the Dodge (and what of the tan car that was too far away to be identified and might simply be going in the same direction?). Or it could be the FBI, the CIA, local law, Andy's group, terrorists, anybody. And did whoever it was follow the Begum only when she was in her limousine or did they also follow plain old Berry Rundle in her cab?

It is also possible that they're following me, she thought. Andy and his merry men to keep an eye on me or to see what I'm up to. Or maybe I have enemies. But why would any enemies of mine follow me? What would they hope to gain by keeping track of my movements?

* * *

BERRY FLUNG BACK her veil. "This thing is stifling me. Funny how it never felt stifling in Gandistan, and it's a lot hotter there."

Because you'd never dare let yourself get drunk in public in Gandistan, Susan thought.

Berry leaned forward and slid open a small panel in the partition that separated them from the driver. She said something in Gandistani into the opening this disclosed. A moment later a blast of icy air rushed into the passenger compartment.

Susan shivered.

Berry took no notice. "What were we talking about? Oh, yes, the deaths in Gandistan. I guess maybe I lied to you a little there, too. You get into the habit of lying when you spend most of your life in a harem. Necessary survival technique."

Whom did she think she was fooling? Berry had been an accomplished liar from the moment she first drew breath. More likely she'd given lessons in deceit to the rest of the harem.

"Okay, so maybe I did shoot a few of my stepsons. But they were awful boys, always trying to kill each other, always trying to kill anyone they felt could get in their way—the prime minister, Sonny, me! I had to kill them, Susan, for Sonny's sake, if not my own, especially after they potted the prime minister. You do understand, don't you?"

Wearily, Susan said once more that she understood. Berry patted her knee again, and this time Susan didn't pull away.

"I knew you would. After all, you are Buck's daughter."

You're going to pay for that, Susan thought between her teeth. She had never thought between her teeth before, but desperate times require desperate measures.

Berry seemed to pull herself together a little, though it was hard to know what was going on behind that burqua. "By the way, I'd appreciate it if you didn't tell any of the gals that I'm the Queen of Gandistan. If your old schoolmates find out you're a queen it makes for strained relations."

She gave another hiccup. "Just ask Queen Noor of Jordan if you don't believe me. I've never met her, but I know how she must feel, being an American gal like me."

"But won't you want to get in touch with all your old friends?" Susan asked, thinking: friends, indeed, they hated your guts. "Since they've all been getting the Rundle House brochures, I took it for granted that meant you were anxious to see them again."

"Of course I'm anxious to see the old gang again. Champing at the bit, in fact. But I'm going to the gala as Berry Rundle. You're the only one who knows my secret, Susan, and the only one who's going to know it. That's because there's a very special relationship between us." And she chuckled drunkenly to herself.

THE LIMOUSINE DREW up in front of Susan's house. The first turbaned man got out and opened the door. "Remember," the Begum said, "you're having dinner with Sonny and me tomorrow night."

The conventional phrase sprang automatically to Susan's lips: "I'm looking forward to it."

"I hope you weren't thinking of bringing that boyfriend of yours along, because he isn't invited."

Susan's voice was as frosty as she could make it. "He wouldn't be able to come in any case, because he isn't in town. He's down in South America."

"For a good long time, I hope. We wouldn't want him to interfere with our plans."

Susan made a noncommittal noise. Peter hadn't given any indication in his last letter of when he planned to return. In fact, now that she thought of it, she hadn't heard from him in weeks. But that often happened when he was in a remote area with poor mail service; silence for a while, then a bunch of letters arriving all at once.

She must remember to get in touch with the young man who was looking after the foundation's affairs in Peter's absence and ask if he'd had any word. What was his name again? She had it written down somewhere.

"I'll call you and we'll work out the details," Berry said. "We'll eat up in my suite. Can't eat in a restaurant because Serwar might be recognized, so I'd have to wear my burqua and it's no fun trying to eat with that on. Don't bother to dress; it'll be quite casual. You won't even need to carry a gun. I promise not to kill you tomorrow night." She laughed heartily.

And I promise not to kill you tomorrow night, Susan thought. She knew through bitter experience that it was not easy to assassinate anyone in the Waldorf and get away with it. Besides, call her sentimental, but she didn't like the idea of assassinating Berry while her son was around, even though, in the long run, she would probably be doing the young man a favor.

"You must remember to tell me when your building is going to be finished," Berry called after her as she got out, "and I'll send you a couple of carpets."

THE TURBANED MAN shut the door of the car and rushed to the entrance of Susan's house in order to open that door as well, but the doorman was before him. No one, he seemed to say, is going to open the door of this house but me.

He glared at the man in the turban. The man in the turban glared at him.

"Ali!" the Begum called.

After a black look at the doorman, Ali reentered the limousine. It drove off.

The doorman continued to hold the door open, but Susan didn't go inside right away. She wanted to see how many cars had been following the limousine. The only vehicles that came by were a small van and two yellow cabs. None of the cars that she thought had been following.

Perhaps the cars that had been following had turned off just before the limousine entered Susan's street, and would pick it up once it started down the avenue. Or they could have been camouflage to cover the van and the cabs which had been the actual followers. Or it was just possible that nobody had been following them at all.

SEVERAL OF THE neighbors had been watching Susan's impressive arrival, mouths agape. Not native New Yorkers; native New Yorkers took such things in their stride. She shouldn't allow the neighbors to get on her nerves like that, Susan told herself.

"My goodness, Susan," said Mrs. Halloran from the fifth floor, a provincial pest who was under the impression that mere residential proximity entitled you to use a person's first name, "who was that interesting lady who brought you home?"

"Mother Teresa," Susan said, and pressed the elevator button.

XVI

"WHAT MAKES YOU so sure that if Berry—the Begum—were out of the picture her son wouldn't just go ahead with the same plan?" Susan asked.

Andy shook his head. "He's not the kind of fellow to do anything like that."

"How can you be so sure?"

"Remember we talked about this before, when I was trying to—er—interest you in the begum? And I haven't given up hope on that."

She shook her head. "Even if I were an assassin, I'd never kill an old classmate."

"Is that a fact?" Andy said. "Now, if I were going to kill someone, some of my old classmates would be among my top choices. But, then, I went to a public school."

Susan was surprised. It was the first time she had seen any evidence of class consciousness from him. Probably he had picked it up from Jill, who had been born and brought up in the Bronx and had never gotten over it.

Susan and Andy were having a late supper in the spacious dining room of her apartment. At first, when the buzzer rang and the doorman's voice informed her that Mr. Mackay was downstairs, she was tempted to tell him to tell Mr. Mackay that she was not at home. She was annoyed with Andy. How could he have put her in this position without telling her what the score was?

Yet she must be fair. He hadn't put her in this position. She had put herself in it. He hadn't suggested that she go to Rundle House; she had gone there of her own volition, without any inkling that Berry Rundle was the Begum of Gandistan, his designated victim.

Andy had undoubtedly known, through Jill if not his own private sources, that Susan would be invited to participate in the Rundle House festivities. What he could not have known was that Berry was going to try to involve her directly in the other, less innocent activities that were going on there.

In any case, it would be stupid to let her annoyance with him keep her from trying to find out as much as she could about what was going on there. "Tell Mr. Mackay he can come up," she said.

Andy arrived smiling, bearing an enormous pizza and a bottle of Chianti. "I know the kind of food they serve at trustees' teas. I figured you might be hungry."

She wondered whether his choice of food were a not-so-subtle allusion to the membership of the board of trustees. Or whether it was simply that he knew she liked pizza.

What did it matter? The pizza smelled good, and she was, indeed, hungry. So she threw together a salad and put out the china and silver and crystal—one must keep up civilized practices—and they sat down at the long mahogany table that Michelle had polished only that morning.

She would have a fit when she discovered that its shining splendor had been dulled by place mats. She always had a fit whenever Susan used the dining room for any but formal occasions. "Don't see why you can't eat in the kitchen like regular folks," she would grumble, "specially when you're eatin' alone, which you're doin' an awful lot of these days."

Susan could not point out to Michelle that she was not "regular folks," because it wasn't the kind of thing you said, even to an employee. According to myth, there were no class distinctions in America.

There were no such myths in Gandistan apparently, although, if the accounts were true, Serwar would have liked to initiate them. "Maybe

111

the king's politics have changed," Susan suggested. "People's ideas do change as they get older. Some people's, anyway," she added, thinking of the king's mother.

"His haven't."

"How do you know?"

"I have information from a reliable source,"

"Who is that?" she asked. "Whom do you have access to who's close enough to him to know what he thinks?"

"I never reveal my sources. You should know better than to ask, Susan."

There was a note of patronage in his voice. She resented it.

"Did your reliable source tell you why he seems to have let his mother take over the country? Surely that would be carrying filial devotion too far."

"That isn't the answer," Andy admitted, "Only thing we've been able to think of is that she must have something on him and she's holding it over his head."

"You mean she might be blackmailing him? Her own son?"

"Such things have been known to happen, especially in royal families."

"But how can you blackmail an absolute monarch? In Gandistan there's nothing he can't do legally—in theory, anyway; and in practice there's nothing he can do that can't be covered up. Unless there's something he did outside of Gandistan . . . ?"

"Not likely that he'd have done something blackmailable here that we wouldn't know about. Besides that, he seems to be a well-conducted young man."

"Then what do you suppose she has on him, if you're right about that?"

"That's what we'd like to know." He looked at her hopefully.

She smiled and helped herself to another piece of pizza. "You hardly think Berry'd be likely to confide in me?" Or that I'd tell you if she had, she thought.

"No, but something might have slipped out in the course of the long chat you two ladies had earlier this evening."

She counted to five. No use getting angry. She'd taken for granted that he and his colleagues had been watching Rundle House. What more likely than that they should have someone on the inside as well, someone who'd reported to him on how long she'd been upstairs with Berry.

"She didn't say anything that could account for it," she told him.

But was that entirely true? She went back over the conversation in her mind. Had Berry let drop anything that could give a clue to the hold she might have over her son? There was the glimmer of . . . something on the edge of Susan's recollection. If only she could pin it down.

"He has a girlfriend somewhere in this area," she offered. "Her name's Audrey. Maybe you could look into her."

"We've already checked her out."

His tone was dismissive. Could Audrey be the informant whose identity he was protecting?

Obviously it would be no use asking him. But Audrey's existence seemed to be no secret. The TV anchorwoman, for instance, seemed to have known about her.

As soon as Susan had a chance, she told herself, she would go to the library and delve into the subject of Gandistan and its ruling family. No need to conceal her interest in the Begum now; it must be already a matter of record. Although it wasn't the Begum she was interested in at the moment. And it might not be necessary to make a trip to the library. She was going to meet Serwar tomorrow night. If he was anything like most young lovers, he was likely to tell her more about Audrey than she wanted to know.

"I suppose you're aware that Berry's keeping her married name a secret. She says she doesn't want anyone to know that she's the Begum of Gandistan, because it would destroy her privacy."

"And she's right. If the media knew that the Begum of Gandistan was an American, they'd be all over her. And it would also attract a lot of attention to Rundle House, which, as you must have gathered by now, the mob is planning to use as a cover."

She knew that whatever was being covered must have something to do with drugs, because of Andy's concern, but she pretended innocence. "A cover for what? Prostitution? White slavery?"

He looked surprised. "Wherever did you get an idea like that? Oh, of course, those girls. No, that would be too obvious. If they wanted a front for a white-slave operation, they'd choose a drug rehabilitation center, something like that. Are you going to eat that last piece of pizza?"

"No, you go ahead and eat it. Meanwhile, I'll make some coffee and see what I can rustle up by way of dessert."

* * *

OVER CHEESE AND crackers and fruit, he gave her a sketchy outline of what was going on, although she felt sure he held back more than he divulged. Since the South American drug cartel seemed to have effectively cornered the cocaine market, he told her, the Mafia, both Sicilian and American, as well as some of the Hong Kong Triads and crime organizations from other countries—"We think even the Turkish Mafia might be involved"—had decided to concentrate their efforts on heroin.

"And heroin is derived from opium, which is Gandistan's chief crop." She was puzzled. "But it's such a small country. Surely their entire opium crop wouldn't be enough to make anything as elaborate as this worthwhile."

"No, it wouldn't. The idea seems to be that the organizers of this thing would centralize their entire heroin manufacturing process in Gandistan—import opium and raw heroin from all over East Asia, and manufacture it with the state-of-the-art technology, like any legitimate big business—which, of course, it would be in Gandistan. They're planning to call it the Gandistan Development Corporation and there'll be a Gandistani national nominally in charge. They've already picked their man. A member of the royal family, of course, someone named Prince Abdul Fuzla. Naturally the Mafia would do the actual running of it."

"I thought there weren't any male members of the royal family left," she said.

"No close ones. He's a cousin of some kind, and a pretty shady character, I understand."

"Where does Rundle House come in?"

"That's going to be their international headquarters."

"But how could they run things from Rundle House? Berry says nobody pays attention to what anyone does in that part of town, and that's probably true when it comes to the neighbors. But it wouldn't apply to law enforcement agencies. They're bound to know about the place, if only by following people like Carlo Battaglia up here."

"So what if they do? Rundle House itself would be used exclusively for administration. All records coded and kept in the computers. They'll be able to hold conferences there without fear of being bugged because they'll own the buildings. And, of course, by getting themselves put on the board of trustees, people like the Bat and Chiang and their associates will have a perfectly legitimate reason to go in and out. And there's nothing the law will be able to do about it. How would it look if law enforcement officials kept getting search warrants and raiding the rooms of underprivileged teen-aged expectant mothers? Imagine what a field day the media would have with it, especially when they don't find a trace of drugs on the premises. And they won't, unless some of the mothers happen to have stashes for their own use, which isn't likely. The Fischetti woman is very strict about things like that. No drugs, no cigarettes, no alcohol."

"You mean she's legitimate?"

"If by legitimate you mean does she really care about unwed teen-aged mothers and their babies, it seems she does. Done a lot of good work in that area, I understand. Very dedicated."

"Don't tell me she doesn't know about this whole drug thing?"

Andy looked exasperated, as if Susan were being deliberately obtuse. "Of course she knows. She's Battaglia's niece, or didn't you know that? But under the new setup, Rundle House will be able to take care of nearly three times as many mothers as they're able to handle now, and they're also planning to open a nursery for the babies. That's all that matters to her."

"Your informant seems to have been working overtime."

"I know all that through the Resource. Our representative on the Metropolitan Charity Council is acquainted with Ms. Fischetti and speaks very highly of her. As a matter of fact, he tells me our outfit has placed quite a few homeless pregnant teen-agers with her, and he was very impressed with the care they got."

It all seemed very well thought out, except for one thing. "Why are they calling attention to Rundle House by holding this big gala?"

"Don't you see? It's to account for the sudden influx of money. Otherwise, how could they explain how Rundle House could suddenly afford to expand like this? The Rundles are rich but not that rich. Actually, they're not attracting all that much attention. Once an organization starts organizing events and sending out press releases and trying to sell tickets, people tend to run when they see them coming."

"Sort of overt covert activities," she said.

"That's one way of looking at it. Did they tell you they were planning to set up branches of Rundle House all over the world?"

"No, they didn't get around to it." She wondered how many charities all over the world were fronts for illegal activities, as well as covert legal ones, like Andy's. It would be a perfect setup for laundering money, if nothing else. From now on, she decided, she would scrutinize the boards of trustees of every organization to which she contributed with an eagle eye.

One thing still puzzled her. "Why do they want me on the board of trustees? Why should they take the risk of having an outsider who might find out what they're up to?"

"They probably didn't think there was much of a risk that you'd catch on," he said, in what she felt was an offensive manner. "And I imagine that they're trying to recruit everyone they can think of who's trustee material, so the board can look more . . . plausible. Not that it would with them on it, but everyone has his blind spots."

Should she tell him that Berry claimed the Bat had joined the board because he had social aspirations? No, he would only laugh. Should she tell him the Bat was supposed to have romantic ideas about Susan herself? No, Andy might have the grace not to laugh, but he would certainly snicker behind his hand. In any case, why should she tell him anything? It was his job to find out things for himself.

XVII

WHEN ANDY ASKED her when she expected to see the Begum again, she said, "Oh, I don't know. Sometime soon, probably." She didn't tell him she'd already agreed to have dinner with the royal family the following evening. If he was so smart, let him find that out for himself—which he probably would.

She spent a restless night being pursued by Berry, who had developed into an Oriental deity with six arms and six hands, each with a gun in it. She woke up with an urge to make a painting of this six-gun goddess, so she got dressed and went over to her studio. These days she had been going there less and less often, as working there was getting to be an unpleasant experience, rather than the uplifting one it should be; but today she was determined to put in at least a few hours' work.

The front door to the loft building where her studio was located stood open, instead of being locked as it should have been when there was no one on duty downstairs—which there hadn't been ever since the new landlord took over and announced that the building was scheduled to be demolished and all the tenants had better get out if they knew what was good for them; although, not being an absolute monarch like Berry, he had couched this threat in less actionable terms.

The downstairs lobby was lit only by a dim bulb, which was sufficient to show that the place was crowded with a miscellany of objects—a couple of discolored sinks, several doors, some worm-eaten lumber, and a number of crushed and mangled cartons, all covered with the grime of ages. Even though it was a warm spring day outside, inside it was chilly and damp; and there was a strong odor of mold and decay and other unpleasant things.

A man was lurking in the shadows near the elevator. She hesitated. He came toward her and she saw that it was only the landlord.

Only the landlord! What mythical monster could compare with the reality of this man! Miss Winkler of Bonnie Buttons had told Susan shortly before she moved to Florida ("I'm too old and too tired to deal with anything but mail order") that she'd heard he had hired thugs to menace the tenants of a building he wanted cleared for demolition. "Of course that was in Queens. I don't think he'd dare try anything like that in Manhattan—at least not on the upper East Side, but one can never be sure."

"Good morning, Mr. Bloodstone," Susan said, coming all the way into the lobby. "It seems to me that service here has been allowed to slip below the limits of acceptability. I'm sure that all this junk—" she prodded a pile of what seemed to be filthy old rags with the toe of her shoe "—is in violation of the fire laws."

"Bonnie and the Frame Master have moved out. That leaves you and Pegasus as the only tenants. Am I expected to keep up full services for only two tenants?"

"Yes, you are."

"If it weren't for you two, I could have the wrecking crew here tomorrow."

"I don't know how long Mr. Pegasus's lease has to run, but mine still has three months to go."

"I offered to buy you out, but I don't suppose money means anything to people like you. And nothing seems to mean anything to Mr. Pegasus."

Mr. Pegasus was a little old Englishman who dealt in objects of an unspecified nature to the antiques trade. In the past, Susan had seen him flitting wraithlike about the halls. From time to time he had leered at her and made what might have been improper suggestions; she couldn't be sure, because the combination of an upper-class British accent and ill-fitting dentures made him almost impossible to understand.

She was not thrilled to discover she would be alone in the building with him for the next three months. She was even less thrilled when Mr. Bloodstone went on, "I'm warning you, the security system isn't as effective as it ought to be because Pegasus turns it off when he comes in and forgets to turn it on again when he leaves."

"The responsibility for keeping the alarm on at all times is yours."

"What am I supposed to do—follow him around? I haven't seen him for days. And he doesn't answer his phone. Maybe he's dead. Though not on the premises," he added hastily. "I checked."

"You're supposed to hire a guard to watch the place while there are still tenants here."

He appeared to think this was intended as a witticism. "You slay me, Miss M., reely you do." He laughed heartily. Then he gave a dramatic start. "Did you see that!" He pointed to the shadows at the back of the hall. "A rat!"

"I didn't see any rat," she said. Except you, she thought. He did look very like a rat with his small beady eyes and his quivering pointed nose. Even his sandy moustache bristled like a rat's whiskers.

"They move very fast. That was a good big one."

"I'm not afraid of rats."

"Very strong-minded of you. Most ladies are terrified of rats. 'Course, there's no reason to be. You leave 'em alone; they leave you alone. Unless, of course, they're very hungry." He grinned. He had pointed teeth like a rat's, too. "Not like people. There are degenerates running around who would do . . . things without any reason. Especially to a woman." He licked his lips. "I hate to think of you alone in a deserted place like this, on the top floor, too. Somebody, anybody, could be lurking in the hallways and on the stairs."

"If the alarm system were on, nobody who didn't belong here would be able to get in."

"Oh, they have their ways. These homeless people are very cunning about getting into abandoned buildings—nearly abandoned buildings—alarm system or not."

"I thought you said it was degenerates who got in."

"Homeless degenerates."

"It's your responsibility to keep them out. My lawyer—"

"Or you could get sick or have an accident up there, and nobody would know for days."

"People know where I am, and I do have a telephone."

"Good, good, I don't want to have to worry about you. Didja hear about the building in Brooklyn that the landlord couldn't start demolishing because there was one tenant who wouldn't leave, and how when somebody from the buildings department came on Monday to inspect the premises, he found a dead body lying in the hall? Looked as if it had been there all weekend; it was already discomposed."

"I heard something about it on the radio. I thought it was the landlord's body they found."

"I understood it was the tenant's."

They smiled at each other with hatred in their hearts—the normal landlord-tenant relationship in New York; perhaps the normal landlord-tenant relationship anywhere.

SHE PRESSED THE elevator button. There was the usual sound of creaking and groaning as the ancient car, roused from its torpor, started bumping its way down the shaft from floor to floor.

"One day the elevator's gonna stop running," Mr. Bloodstone's voice said in her ear. "Maybe it'll even stop between floors, and it'll be hours before anyone finds anyone who happens to be stuck in it. Days maybe. Oh, the elevator alarm's working . . . but there won't be anybody to hear it."

The elevator door opened. She went inside.

"The building could catch on fire!" he yelled after her. "Burn to the ground. With all your beautiful paintings inside."

"They're fully insured," she told him, as she pulled the elevator door shut.

No need to mention that only the paintings she was currently working on were in the studio. The bulk of her output was safely stored in a fireproof warehouse in Long Island City. That had been Jill's idea. Susan could see now it was a good one.

This building might be a good place to dispose of Berry, she thought, as the elevator wobbled its way up to the top floor. No one to see her go in; no one to see her not go out, as long as Susan chose her time carefully. Mr. Bloodstone never appeared except in the morning. Afternoons he went out to persecute tenants in Brooklyn and Queens before going home to his palatial estate on Long Island.

There should be no difficulty in luring Berry here on the pretext of showing her Susan's paintings. Although it might be difficult to persuade her to come alone. This was near First Avenue, well beyond what Berry seemed to consider the safety zone, although it was still a high-rent area.

Suppose she did manage to get Berry up to the studio alone and killed her? What was she going to do with the body? Even if she could get her out of the studio and into the elevator—and, with a heavyweight like Berry, that was no small task—what then? She couldn't leave it in the lobby; it would be too easy to establish a connection between Susan Melville and Berengaria Rundle. The thought crossed her mind that in a pinch she could call on Andy for removal—but, no, he might expect a reciprocal courtesy. She didn't want to put herself under any obligation to him.

Then, of course, there was the possibility—the very remote possibility —that, if she tried to shoot Berry, Berry would shoot her first. Berry would have no trouble getting rid of the body. She'd just have her attendants bring a carpet, roll the corpse in it, and carry it to the limousine; then up to Rundle House, where there would be complete removal facilities, courtesy of the Bat and his henchmen. Would he reproach Berry for having killed her? Would he shed a silent—or noisy—tear on her behalf?

What does it matter, she told herself sternly. Besides, Berry could never outshoot me. She's too fat.

She unlocked the door to her studio and went inside. Andy had told her the night before that Jill wanted to get in touch with her. She'd call her now. She picked up the phone. The line was dead. No dial tone, no humming sound, no tiny distant voices. Nothing.

Suddenly she was no longer in a mood to paint. She would go out, do something else. Shop, perhaps. She did need a new handbag. Her bags wore out quickly. The weight of a gun, no matter how light, tended to take a toll on their seams, especially dress bags, and most of her assassinations were dressy affairs.

She could, of course, have a bag specially made. But how could she explain her needs to the bag maker?

On the other hand, as Berry had pointed out, today women in all walks of life carried guns for self-protection. Perhaps handbags especially designed for gun-toters were already on the market. She remembered having seen an ad for a catalogue of such merchandise when she'd turned out her drawers looking for the Rundle House brochure.

121

She'd always meant to send away for it and had never gotten around to it. She would make a point of sending for it as soon as she got back home.

She locked the studio door behind her; then paused, reluctant to take the elevator. The building was only seven stories high. Walking downstairs would be no problem. But she had a feeling that she would meet Mr. Bloodstone on the way and he would smirk at her and say, "I hope I didn't frighten you into using the stairs, Miss M. Or were you just walking down for the exercise?"

Why should she let him get to her? She opened the door marked "Exit," and looked down the stairwell. Pitch black. All the light bulbs had been allowed to go out. Or had been removed. Something rustled on the stairs.

She took the elevator. It rattled and clanked, but it arrived at the ground floor. Mr. Bloodstone was still in the lobby, bending over the corpse of a large gray rat.

He jumped when he saw her. "I got it right after you went up. I was just about to get rid of it."

Oh, sure, she thought. You didn't expect me back down so soon, did you? You were going to leave it there, hoping it would scare me.

Probably he hadn't seen a rat at all before, she thought. Probably he had brought this one along with him. Very likely it had died of natural causes.

"I hope you're going to give it a decent burial," she said, resisting the temptation to add, "in your family plot."

Now, if she wanted to kill Mr. Bloodstone—if she were *planning* to kill Mr. Bloodstone; she wanted to kill him all right—there wouldn't be any problem. No one would question the appearance of a landlord's body on his own premises. Moreover, the death wasn't likely to be associated with her any more than with any of his other tenants, past and present. The field would be wide open.

But she had promised herself that from now on, she would keep from giving in to her lethal impulses. She had already killed one landlord on impulse. And it was true that his demise had brought her out of poverty and eventually opened the way to fame and fortune. But the second time, she told herself, she might not be as lucky.

THERE WAS NO reason for her to keep on suffering. She would go to one of the many real estate offices in the neighborhood and see if she could rent studio space for a few months. She knew it would make Mr. Bloodstone happy, but she couldn't sacrifice her comfort for his pain.

She needn't have worried. It turned out to be impossible to find anything in the neighborhood to suit her needs. "You might be able to find something in the financial district or in Soho," the agent suggested. "Maybe even the Twenties or Thirties. But, even so, for just a few months . . ."

"I'd be willing to sign a lease for a year." Even if the work on the Melville building got done in the three months that had been promised, it probably would be several months more before she'd actually be able to move in. "But I want space in this neighborhood. I like to walk to work. Aren't there any subleases available?"

The agent would have sneered if Susan hadn't been such an important person. She shrugged instead. "Well, we'll keep an eye out. But frankly I can't hold out much hope. Now, if you'd like a nice condominium . . . ?"

XVIII

S<small>USAN COULD TRY</small> other agents, but she knew they would say the same thing. She could go back to painting in her apartment, the way she'd done before she became affluent again. But now that she'd had the place renovated (and that had taken more than twice as long as promised) she would hate to have it all stained and smeared with paint. And Michelle would have fits.

Susan didn't need to paint for a livelihood. She could easily stop painting until the Melville Building was ready for occupancy. She could easily stop painting for the rest of her life. The warehouse was crammed with enough paintings, which Jill was letting out one by one for fear of depressing the market, so that she would never need to lift a brush again. Moreover, Jill had made a number of excellent investments for Susan. So, if the art market crashed, if the threatened recession materialized, Susan would still be a wealthy woman.

But she needed to keep on painting because it was what defined her, made her Susan Melville, not only in the eyes of the world but, more important, in her own eyes. And she supposed that she kept on disposing of evil-doers for much the same reason, even though that defined her only in her own eyes (and perhaps in Andy's eyes, too, although she supposed he did not see it as a matter of definition).

SHE WENT OVER to the Melville Foundation to see how matters were progressing. They did not seem to have progressed at all. Mr. Iverson had suffered a nervous breakdown, the foreman told her. There was a distinct suggestion of cause and effect. She wasn't sure whether he was joking or not. Construction humor? Maybe she should call Mr. Pilokis, the contractor. No, she'd call Jill. Ask her to call Mr. Pilokis. Give him a nervous breakdown, too, if that was what was necessary to get things done.

She had lunch by herself at a little place over on Second Avenue that she had discovered on one of her outings with Jill. Then she went to Bloomingdale's, since it was handy, to check out their bags. She couldn't bring herself to ask whether they had any bags specially designed for gun-carrying. Maybe at Macy's, but not Bloomingdale's. So she bought herself an ordinary but sturdy one.

Since she had time on her hands, she took a little of it to explore Bloomingdale's. Each time she went there it seemed to have changed. Now it was more of a sound and light show than a department store. Nothing seemed to be left of the original façade, except for a rather sinister bit on the north side that had been relegated to entrances for employees and deliveries. All the rest of the building had been given a false face.

Bloomingdale's had always been a regular rabbit warren of a place, with numerous entrances on all four sides, elevators and escalators and mezzanines and basements and subbasements. She was surprised to see that there were still entrances to the subway in the subbasements. She wouldn't have thought that Bloomingdale's catered to the subway crowd any more. But, then, they did hold sales, as the little banks of TV screens at the head of every escalator were constantly reminding you.

The customers seemed divided among young women who looked like hookers (yuppies) and middle-aged women who looked like bag ladies (old money), with a sprinkling of overly well-dressed young men and men trying to look young, plus people who would blend into any crowd but this one.

Although there were still aisles on the main floor, much of the rest of the store had been divided up into clusters and "boutiques," so that it

125

was more of a rabbit warren then before—a warren for trendy, well-heeled rabbits. What an ideal spot for an assassination it was! She wouldn't even need to use a silencer. There was so much noise from the music that was continually being played that the sound of a shot was not likely to be heard, or, if it was heard, to be noticed.

It shouldn't be hard to lure Berry there. By her own admission, she was an ardent shopper. And she had mentioned Lexington Avenue as one of her stamping grounds. What else was there on Lexington Avenue but Bloomingdale's? Yes, it was definitely the place for her to get Berry. She would come back tomorrow and reconnoiter the ground carefully, study the little maps posted on each floor for the benefit of hapless shoppers who had lost their way in the maze. She didn't think she could take any more of it today. Bloomingdale's was an experience you had to prepare for, if not with fasting at least with prayer.

As SUSAN OPENED the door to her apartment, a wave of perfume engulfed her. The place was filled with flowers, masses of them in baskets and bowls and vases, even one arrangement that looked like a wreath, spilling out of the living room into the foyer in a riot of color. And, in the midst of all this floral abundance, Michelle's grinning face. "Looks like somebody's got herself a new beau."

"Don't be silly, Michelle, they must have come from Mr. Peter."

But Peter was not accustomed to express his affection with botanic displays. Even in the early days, when they had been more ardently involved, his love tokens had taken the form of a shrunken head here, a bunch of poisoned arrows there. He had never said it with flowers.

"Mr. Peter!" Michelle made a rude noise with her tongue. She had never approved of Peter. "These're from some fellow named Carlo. 'Your devoted Carlo,' he signs hisself. Such a romantic name, Carlo."

"Michelle, you had no right to read the card."

"The public has a right to know and I'm the public!" And Michelle stomped off before Susan could say anything further.

If only Michelle knew what Carlo's last name was, who Carlo himself was, Susan thought, she wouldn't think his name was so romantic. Or maybe she would. Maybe it would give her new respect for her employer.

Susan supposed she would have to call the Bat and thank him for the flowers. Or would a thank-you-note be more appropriate? She would decide later. Meanwhile what was she going to do with all this botanical extravagance?

She'd take them to her studio, use them as models. Then she remembered how little the atmosphere of her studio was conductive to painting now. Maybe she'd ask Jill to find out from Mr. Pilokis whether it might be possible to finish the studio on the top floor first. Then she could work there while they were doing the rest of the building. It might be noisy but it wouldn't be creepy.

AT AROUND FOUR, a male voice with a foreign accent called and said the Begum's limousine would pick her up at seven-thirty, if that would be convenient. Susan said that would be quite convenient.

What to wear? She contemplated her wardrobe. It was important to dress in such a way as to show she did not regard the occasion as anything special without compromising her own sense of what was fitting. Finally she decided on basic black with . . . pearls? No, pearls—even fake pearls—were too corny.

A simple gold chain and earrings? Of course, the first rule of living in New York is never to go out in the city wearing visible gold jewelry. But she wouldn't be going out in the literal sense. She would be stepping out of a well-staffed apartment house and into a well-guarded limousine. From that limousine, she would be stepping into the Waldorf Astoria. If, to paraphrase the words of the song, you were not safe from chain-snatchers there, you were not safe anywhere.

Michelle came in to inform Susan that she was leaving and to ask whether she could take some of the flowers home with her. "Otherwise, you're likely to get sfixiated, you got so many of 'em." It wasn't until she'd reached the door that she remembered to tell Susan that there had been a number of calls for her while she was out. "This time I left a list by the phone like you tole me to," she said virtuously. "Have a nice time."

"Nice time?"

"Thought you said sumpin' 'bout goin' out to dinner tonight when you give me that dress to press. And, if you ask me, it's more fitten for a funeral. Anyways, give him my love."

"Give whom your love?"

"This Carlo. Ain't he the one you're going out to dinner with?"

"I'm going out to dinner with an old school friend."

"And you went to an all-girls' school, right? In that case, the dress is perfeck."

There was, indeed, a list by the phone, but, as far as Susan could tell from Michelle's scrawl, it was a laundry list. Unless Susan's callers had consisted of individuals variously named Sheets, Towels, Pillowcases, and something she could not decipher at all. There were figures that looked like telephone numbers but seemed to bear no relationship to anything else. Michelle must have gotten the two lists mixed up. Or figured her employer would be able to tell from the phone numbers who her callers had been. But none of the numbers was familiar. Oh, well, Susan thought, if any of the calls were important, they'll call again.

THE LIMOUSINE ARRIVED precisely at seven twenty-nine. "Good evening," the turbaned man said, as he opened the car door for her. So he spoke English. But, of course, some of Berry's entourage must speak English. The man on the phone, for example. Unless he'd been someone from the Waldorf.

Susan entered the car, observed by a small group of neighbors who seemed to have sprung up out of nowhere. If only the contractor would get a move on and finish the whole building, so she could get out of this place. Maybe if she dropped a word in Carlo Battaglia's ear, he would be able to rush things. She'd heard he had influence in the construction industry.

But you couldn't ask a man a favor and then kill him. Did she really want to kill him? Was he really that much worse than Mr. Bloodstone?

XIX

A WOMAN IN Gandistani garb admitted Susan to the royal suite, where the Begum and the king awaited her. The suite was standard Waldorf luxury, plus a few Oriental touches which the Gandistanis had presumably brought along with them to give the place a homey touch. There was the same spicy odor of incense she had smelled up in Berry's boudoir, although she saw no signs of an actual incense burner. Perhaps it was against fire department regulations.

Berry was resplendent in a crimson and gold garment, adorned with rubies and diamonds in all probable places plus a few improbable ones. This time there was an out-and-out tiara on her head. "It'll be quite casual," she'd said. Perhaps this was casual for Gandistan.

The young king wore a business suit. No turban. No beard or moustache, either. He looked much as he had in the photograph, except thinner and older, and what hadn't been evident in the picture was obvious now. His eyes were blue. As they had been in Susan's dream.

Susan looked at Berry to see if she had developed two additional pairs of arms to match Susan's other dream. She seemed to have only one pair, but there could easily be several more concealed beneath her voluminous dress.

Stop being fanciful, Susan told herself. She's not some mysterious Oriental. She's only Berry Rundle.

Both Serwar and his mother looked flushed and angry, as if Susan's arrival had interrupted a heated argument. Even royal families had their differences, Susan supposed, but she hoped they wouldn't continue their quarrel while she was there. Always so difficult for a guest to feel comfortable while a family quarrel raged around her.

The king shook hands with her. His grip was firm. "Delighted to meet you, Miss Melville," he said in a pleasant baritone.

He didn't look delighted. Does he have something against me? Susan wondered. Could Berry have told him something to prejudice him? Or was he simply sulky about having to spend an evening entertaining one of his mother's friends?

On the other hand, he was a king. Kings ought to be accustomed to spending a large part of their time entertaining people who bored them.

No, Susan thought, he disapproves of me specifically.

She was intrigued. No one had ever disapproved of her before.

"Would you like a drink, Susan?" the Begum asked. "Sonny and I are prohibited by Islamic law from touching alcohol, so we're sticking to fruit juice, but there's no reason why you shouldn't have a regular drink."

"Oh, come off it, Mother. Everyone in Gandistan knows you drink like a fish."

"You're just saying that to hurt me. I may take a little drink from time to time, but I've always taken great care to be discreet."

Serwar gave a short, sharp laugh. His mother puffed angrily at her cigarette. Her holder this time was of carved white jade.

Before Susan had a chance to say she would be perfectly happy with fruit juice, another Gandistani woman glided in bearing a tray that held a bottle of sherry—apparently considered an appropriate preprandial beverage for a genteel infidel—with one glass and a plate of canapés. She was followed by the first woman carrying another tray with a glass pitcher containing a rather noxious-looking orange liquid and two glasses, as well as another plate of canapés.

Both set down their burdens and left with choreographic precision. There should have been music, Susan thought. At least a gong.

Serwar sipped at his sherry with obvious distaste. "Don't you have something stronger secreted on the premises, Mother?"

"Not now, Sonny," she said.

"Mother is always so concerned with appearances," he said to Susan. "Do you, too, worry about appearances, Miss Melville?"

"Don't call her Miss Melville," Berry interposed. "Call her—um—call her Aunt Susan."

Susan gave her a dirty look.

Serwar laughed. "I'm curious about you, Miss Melville," he went on, "because you're the only friend—the only American friend—of Mother's I've ever met, and I wondered what her friends were like. Did she have a lot of friends when she was growing up here in New York?"

Susan refused to be drawn into the royal differences. "She was very popular," she lied.

"You'll meet a lot of my friends at the Rundle House gala," Berry told her son. "Then you can see what they're like for yourself."

"I told you I was not going to that gala. And I don't see how you can possibly expect me to. My face, even without whiskers, is known to some of the media. If you introduce me as your son, everybody will know who you are."

A wave of Berry's cigarette holder sent ashes all over her rubies and diamonds. She brushed them off with a jeweled hand. "But I'm not going to introduce you as my son. Think I'm a fool? You are going to go with Susan, and she's going to introduce you as her royal patron. What's more, you are going to go to the opening of her show in the fall—"

"Only if you want to," Susan interrupted.

"Oh, I don't mind," he sighed. "I go to so many of those things, one more . . . ." And he shrugged. "I suppose I'll have to be the guest of honor, unless," he added hopefully, "you're also inviting the king of a large country or a president or prime minister."

"I'm afraid Jill will expect you to be the guest of honor," Susan apologized. "Jill is my manager and very concerned with what she fancies to be my best interests."

She is also, she thought, the wife of a secret agent who is taking a very unfriendly interest in your mother, and who will also be at the opening. But by that time, she told herself, it shouldn't make any difference.

Berry chuckled. "I've heard about this Jill. Really rubbed the Fish the wrong way, didn't she? Better not let her come near Carlo, though, if you value her health."

131

Miss Melville Rides a Tiger

* * *

BERRY FINISHED THE sherry in her glass, as well as the contents of one of the plates of canapés, on which she had been nibbling ever since they arrived. "I've been telling Sonny how much New York has changed since I used to live here."

"I've been here before, Mother. I know that it's changed."

"You never set eyes on New York until ten years ago. I was born here!"

She turned to Susan. "I hadn't seen it since I left the country until about six years or so ago, when the old man started to fail and I was able to get away from time to time. Believe you me, it was a shock. Double-decker buses gone, Penn Station gone, the Astor gone. Remember how we used to meet our friends under the clock at the Astor, Susie? No, you were too young."

So should you have been, Susan thought. One did not meet people of the same sex under the clock at the Astor.

"Before that, for over thirty years I was practically a prisoner. I could get magazines and newspapers from abroad. I could order anything I wanted from abroad. I lived in a marble palace with—with—"

"Vassals and serfs at your side," Susan suggested.

"That was the trouble. I couldn't get them to leave my side. I couldn't get away from Gandistan."

"Why should you have wanted to get away?" Serwar asked. "Gandistan's an earthly paradise; isn't that what you've been telling those new business associates of yours?"

"For their purposes it is. They won't find a better place in the world to do business."

"To do their kind of business. Oh, I agree to that. Don't you, Miss Melville?"

She didn't know what to say. Fortunately, the question seemed to be rhetorical, because, without waiting for an answer, he picked up the sherry bottle and looked at her. When she shook her head, he poured more sherry in his own glass.

Berry took the bottle from his hand and filled her own now-empty glass to the brim again. Apparently she didn't worry about her attendants smelling her breath in the Waldorf.

Susan tried to shift to a neutral topic. "What's the climate of Gandistan like?"

132

"Terrible," Berry answered. "Hot and sticky most of the time, with nasty little black flies that go after you in a very purposeful way."

She seemed to recollect that she was supposed to be a Gandistan booster. "Up in the hills it's quite cool, though. A lot of people go there in summer to escape the heat and, of course, the floods. But it's all absolutely unspoiled. No overdevelopment, no pollution."

"Not yet," Serwar said.

Once again Susan tried to change the subject. "You speak remarkably good English, your majesty. I know you went to university here, but—"

"Still, I should have some sort of accent, eh? Well, don't forget I am half American. And all my tutors were either American or English. Please don't call me your majesty; it makes me uncomfortable."

"Yes, your—er—Serwar." If he'd had an English royal name, like Charles or Philip, it would have been easier. She couldn't bring herself to call him Sonny.

"Besides that, my grandfather didn't speak any language but English. My maternal grandfather, that is. My paternal grandfather died—of unnatural causes, like most of the rulers of Gandistan—long before I was born." He sighed, as if he were wondering what his own chances of dying a natural death would be.

"My father lived in Gandistan till the end of his life," Berry explained. "He was great pals with my husband. They used to . . . engage in all kinds of sports together."

"What happened to him? Susan asked.

Serwar opened his mouth.

"He died of a fever," Berry said, a little too quickly. "It must've been —um—around fifteen years ago. You were thirteen, weren't you, Sonny?"

He nodded.

"Yes, fifteen years. We gave him a lovely funeral. Remember his funeral, Sonny, wasn't it lovely? I will say this for my late husband, he really knew how to throw a funeral."

"I would have thought you'd have had your father's body shipped back to the United States to be put in the family vault."

"The family didn't want him alive; they didn't get him dead," Berry said. "Besides, he expressed a desire to be buried in Gandistan." But she avoided Susan's eye, as she spoke.

"Your Majesty—" Susan began, after a moment of respectful silence.

"I told you, call me Serwar. Otherwise, I'll call you Aunt Susan."

133

"Serwar, I happened to see you get off the plane the other day."

He looked surprised. "You were there? At the airport?"

"No, no, I mean I saw you on television that evening."

"Ah, yes, the ubiquitous TV cameras. I noticed them but I hadn't realized I'd gotten on the evening news."

"You were wearing a beard and moustache. And you're clean-shaven now . . . ?" She stopped, wondering whether the question had been too personal.

He laughed. "No, I did not come here in disguise. Nor am I in disguise now. I shaved my beard and moustache off as soon as I got here. Audrey doesn't like them. Audrey, as I suppose my mother has told you, is my fiancée."

"Audrey's your girlfriend. You don't have a fiancée." His mother poured a little more sherry into her son's glass and a lot more into hers, which emptied the bottle. If the staff of the Waldorf thinks I'm the only one who drank the sherry, Susan thought, then they're going to think I'm a souse.

"You're probably thinking that Sonny doesn't need my permission to get married; he's the sultan. And you're right. As long as his bride is a Moslem—or converts to Islam, the way I did—" here she gave her son a peculiar smile "—nobody can interfere. After all, nobody stopped Sonny's dad from marrying me, did they?"

Serwar looked furious. "Mother, must you wash our dirty linen in public?"

"I'm sure Audrey would be gratified to hear herself referred to as 'dirty linen.' Not that it isn't an appropriate description for—"

"*Mother!*" Serwar said warningly. Apparently he would stick up for the woman he loved, even if he wouldn't stick up for his country.

"And Susan isn't public," she went on, waving her cigarette holder. A shower of sparks fell on her ample bosom.

"Be careful, Mother," Serwar said, as he helped her brush them off. "If you set fire to the place once more, royalty or not, we're never going to be allowed into the Waldorf again."

She ignored him. "Susan is my oldest and dearest . . . friend. We were practically brought up together. We even think alike in many ways."

Now what does she mean by that? Susan wondered. Is it an insult? A threat? A warning?

Berry wiped away a tear that was plowing a furrow in her makeup. "Her father was the only man I ever loved. Your father was a good

134

man, Sonny, but I never loved him. Oh, who's kidding who? He was a monster and I hated him. But I loved Buck Melville."

Serwar looked from Susan to Berry and then back again. "I knew there had been some romance in your life before you married my father. Heaven knows, you've talked about it often enough. But . . . Miss Melville's *father*?"

"Your mother had a crush on my father when she was fifteen," Susan said quickly. "You know how schoolgirls are. It didn't mean anything."

"It meant a lot," Berry said hotly, "to him as well as me. You knew it then, Susan Melville, and you know it now. You just won't—"

The woman who had let them in appeared in the doorway and said something in Gandistani.

"Dinner seems to be ready," Serwar said. "And high time, too."

XX

BERRY ROSE AND, waving her cigarette holder like a baton, led the way into an adjacent dining room, where there was a table set for three. Here there was music, but it was Mozart, nothing Oriental. Susan wondered whether this was Berry's or her son's choice? Most likely it was the Waldorf's.

The Gandistani woman bowed and left.

"We're going to dine en famille," Berry said. "Serve ourselves. That way we'll be able to talk. You never know how much English they understand."

The food, which had been laid out on a side table, appeared to have come from the Waldorf's kitchens, so it was standard haute cuisine, with no exotic Gandistani touches. Susan was thankful. During her previous sorties into United Nations circles, she had had enough experience with the various cuisines of Southeast Asia to last her a lifetime. The table settings were obviously the Waldorf's, except for a huge bulbous decoration of gilded (or, possibly, gold) metal, which was too hideous to be part of the hotel's service. It had to belong to Berry.

There was wine, too, presumably for Susan's exclusive consumption, since her place setting was the only one that held a wine glass. Was Berry under the impression that the servants would think Susan had been able to get through three bottles of Bordeaux all by herself?

"Why do you go on with this charade, Mother?" the young king asked, as he poured water into his and his mother's water goblets. Nobody thinks you're strictly observant. Our people all know you wear Western clothes when you go shopping."

"Wearing Western clothes is one thing. Drinking alcohol is another."

He made a little hissing sound between his teeth, just like his mother, Susan thought. Pity he wasn't more like her in strength of character, but she wouldn't wish any other of his mother's character traits upon him.

"Speaking of going out shopping," Berry said to Susan, "I'm planning to go to Bloomingdale's again with Lucy tomorrow. Not that she's the companion I'd choose if I had my druthers. She got sick when we were there this morning, and I had to send for someone to take her home. But I don't know anyone else in these parts anymore. I guess the Fish would go if I asked her, but she's not the kind of gal you'd want to go shopping with."

"I thought you liked to go shopping alone, as plain old Berry Rundle," Susan said.

"Well, I do, but it's always more fun when you're with someone."

She took a second generous helping of pâté. "Now, Bloomingdale's is one of the few places in New York that's changed for the better. Remember what a dowdy old place it used to be? And look at it now. World famous for its sh-chic."

She had trouble pronouncing the word. The wine was beginning to get to her. Not that, Susan suspected, the sherry had been her first drink of the evening.

Berry hiccuped. "I must say I was really impressed by the place. It's like no other store in the world, their slogan says, and I believe it. As soon as things really get going in Gandistan, I'm going to see if we can't arrange to get a department store like that for Sultanabad."

Serwar appeared to choke on his wine. He wasn't eating much, Susan noticed. She didn't feel much like eating herself, but she made an effort to put up a good show in order to demonstrate to Berry that she was entirely at ease.

"Maybe you would like to come to Bloomingdale's with me tomorrow, Susan?"

* * *

THAT THING IN the middle of the table must be a magic lamp, Susan thought—even more magical than the one in *The Arabian Nights* because she hadn't even had to rub it to get her wish. Hadn't she been thinking only that afternoon what a perfect place Bloomingdale's would be in which to despatch Berry and wondering how she would lure her there. And now—presto!—Berry was inviting her to go shopping with her.

It couldn't simply be a coincidence. The genie of the bulbous thing must be on Susan's side. Perfectly understandable if he was a Gandistani genie.

All the same, Susan wished she could have another day or two in which to explore the terrain and plan her strategy. She had been thinking of getting a camera and photographing the maps on each floor so she could work out her campaign at home. Pity to give up her plans.

She tried stalling. "I'd love to go with you. Trouble is, I promised myself I was going to spend the whole day tomorrow painting. I find it's very important to structure your life when you work on your own. Otherwise it tends to get—uh—unstructured. Couldn't we make it later in the week? Or, better yet, next week?"

"I'm afraid it has to be tomorrow. There are some things I need that I didn't have a chance to pick up today, because of Lucy. I know I could have tradesmen come up here and show me their wares, but then I might just as well be back in Gandistan."

Sometimes overplanning could wreck a campaign. Many of Susan's best killings had been played by ear. "Oh, I suppose I could take tomorrow off and go with you. After all, we haven't seen each other for so many years."

"That's big of you," Berry said. "I promise I'll make it up to you."

"I'm sure you will," Susan said.

Serwar looked bewildered. "Is there something here I'm missing?"

"Just girl talk," his mother said. "Maybe you'd like to come with us, Sonny?"

"I'd rather be dead."

"Men always hate to go shopping," his mother told Susan. Susan wondered on what life experience Berry based this observation. Had she been unable to drag her late husband, the supreme ruler of Gandistan to the bazaar? Had the eunuchs turned petulant when asked to pick up a few things at the market?

Berry pushed a cigarette into her holder, and lit it, after several tries. Her son made no attempt to light it for her. "Mother, I wish you wouldn't smoke while we're eating."

"If wishes were watches, they would be fried," Berry said thickly, and hiccuped.

Serwar said something in Gandistani that sounded distinctly unfilial.

THERE FOLLOWED ONE of those awkward silences that so often fall in the middle of a social gathering. Susan felt it was up to her, as the representative of Western civilization, to break it. "Since you seem to have been so favorably impressed by Bloomingdale's, Berry, are you going to recommend it to Mr. Battaglia as a good buy?"

Berry looked uncomprehending. So did her son. "Your mother was talking to me yesterday about his buying it," Susan explained. "She says it's for sale."

"That's right," Berry nodded. "He's looking to buy into some up-scale enterprise."

"But Bloomingdale's! The Bat's thinking of buying Bloomingdale's! I don't believe it!"

"No doubt it's Audrey's favorite store," Berry said.

"Audrey does all her shopping at discount stores. She says it's the politically correct thing to do."

"A fine queen she'd make, I don't think," his mother sneered.

Even though there were probably no discount stores in Gandistan, it did seem an unregal attitude. "What does Audrey do?" Susan asked. Obviously a young woman who shopped only in discount stores and was politically correct was not likely to be a lily of the field.

"She works for the Coalition of Oppressed Minorities Everywhere. As a paid employee, not a volunteer," he added. There was a distinct note of smugness in his voice. He had spent at least five years in the United States, Susan reminded herself. Plenty of time to pick up these activist attitudes.

"Big deal," his mother observed, shaking ashes all over the table. She took a second helping of braised duck and all the rest of the herbed potatoes.

"Why, I know COME," Susan said. "I spoke at their auction of art by displaced Transylvanians last year, and I met a number of their people. I wonder if Miss—?"

"Skeat, Audrey Skeat. She says she met you."

"The name doesn't ring a bell," Susan apologized.

"Tall, thin girl who looks like a horse and brays like a donkey," Berry said helpfully.

Serwar started to say something; then thought better of it.

Susan gave up representing Western civilization, and was silent.

"SINCE THIS IS a special occasion, I have something very special here." Berry lifted off the top of the bulbous thing and pulled out a bottle of Courvoisier with the air of a magician pulling a rabbit out of a hat. "Oh, drat, we've already used the water glasses!"

"I'm sure there must be other glasses in the serving pantry," her son said. "If you're worried about the staff, you can always wash the glasses and put them back afterward."

"I am a queen," Berry said. "I do not do washing up."

Serwar made the little family hissing sound between his teeth; then got up and came back with three glasses. He set one at each place. He was very obliging for a king, Susan thought. Too obliging, in fact. Audrey's influence, no doubt.

"No brandy for me, thank you," Susan said. "I've drunk too much wine as it is, and I'm beginning to feel a trifle sleepy."

"No brandy for me, either," Serwar said. "I'll probably be going out for a drive after dinner."

"To see Audrey, I suppose," his mother said.

"Perhaps."

"Then why did you get three glasses if you weren't going to drink?"

"I don't know. I suppose I didn't think."

"You never think," she said. "That's your trouble. One of your troubles. Very well, then, I shall drink alone." And, lifting her glass in the air in pantomime salute, she tossed off her brandy. She set down her glass. "I wonder what your cousin Abdul would think of Audrey."

"I don't give a damn what Cousin Abdul would think of Audrey," Serwar said.

Abdul . . . the man who was going to be the titular head of the operation in Gandistan was called Abdul something or other; probably the same man, since Andy had said he was a cousin. But why should his opinion of Audrey matter?

"Aren't you going to eat your dessert, Susan?" Berry asked.

"I'm too full to eat anything more."

So should Berry have been. In addition to eating most of the canapés before they even sat down, she'd cleared everything on her plate and finished what was left in the serving platters. Now she lifted Susan's dessert dish to her place. "Build a better moussetrap and the world will beat a mousse to your door. And don't look at me like that. I'm not worried about my cholesterol. In fact, I don't believe there is such a thing as cholesterol. Just something those food fascists made up. And I'm not going to an exercise saloon—salon, either."

Serwar looked surprised. "Did Miss Melville suggest that you go to an exercise salon?"

"No, my beloved little shishter—sister, Lucy did."

"You know you never pay any attention to what Aunt Lucy says. Why pay attention to her now?"

"It hurts when your own kith—whatever that means—and kin think you're too fat, even when they're an idiot. You don't think I'm too fat, do you, Sonny?"

"No, Mother, I think you're perfect."

"You're being sus-sarcastic. You don't 'preshiate all I've done for you, and I'm going to do for you. Hospitals, schools, libraries, everything you've always said you wanted."

"Not everything," he said. "Not by a long shot."

XXI

He turned to Susan. "Did you meet your fellow board members yesterday? And I don't mean my mother's relatives. I suppose you must have known them from before."

"They're your relatives, too, Sonny. Your own kin and kith. Kith me, kith me again," Berry sang to herself in an undertone.

"That's unfortunately true." He shook his head. "Maybe Audrey's right in refusing to marry me. My genes are nothing to write home about."

"But I thought . . . ?"

"Oh, it's Audrey who won't marry me. If she'd say yes, I wouldn't care what Mother or anyone said; I'd marry her right away."

"Oh, you would, would you!" Berry said. "Jush you try and shee how far it gets you." She hiccuped.

She's really disgusting, Susan thought.

"What I meant, of course," Serwar said, "is that I'd marry her if she'd agree to convert."

"That's ri'," Berry said. "If she won't convert, you can't marry her.

142

Royal resh—reshponsibility. When the time comes, I will pick you a nishe wife. In Gandistan," she explained to Susan, "marriages are always arranged. Mush the bes' way."

Serwar pretended to ignore her. "When I said 'fellow board members' I was referring to the non-Rundle members of the board."

"You mean those gangsters?"

"That's just what I do mean. Are they the kind of people you'd feel comfortable associating with?"

Berry frowned. Apparently her son was committing something that in anyone other than the king would be *lèse-majesté*. "Have you heard about Carlo and Susan?" she asked him. "Quite a little romansh there. Like you and Audrey. But with a happier ending, I trusht."

"The Bat and Miss Melville! You said something about that before, but I thought you were joking."

"She is joking," Susan said. "She's a great little kidder; she said so herself."

Berry shook her head. "I kid you not. He met her years ago at a wedding, and he's carried her image in his heart ever since." She heaved a sigh which might not have been mock. She was so drunk she could have been sincerely maudlin.

"Your mother is exaggerating. I was at that wedding and I suppose I must have met him, although I don't remember it. He apparently remembers me. And that's all there is to it."

"You're too modesht," Berry said. "How could anyone forget you? I certainly never did."

She got to her feet unsteadily. " 'Scuse me, mus' go to the little girls' room. Too much fruit juice." She staggered out of the room.

"Poor mother," Serwar said. "I suppose in some ways she's led a difficult life. Gandistan is no place for a Western woman."

"And an Eastern woman?"

"Eastern women are at least used to it, although conditions are changing for them in most countries, and I hope they will in Gandistan, too."

"It's up to you, isn't it?" Susan asked.

"Ah, but even a king must answer to a higher power," he said. She wasn't sure whether he was referring to his God or his mother.

"MAYBE I WILL have some brandy, after all," Serwar said. "Sure you won't change your mind?"

She shook her head.

He poured brandy into his glass, but, instead of drinking, he looked into the depths of the liquid as if he saw some kind of vision of the future there. If he did, it was not a happy one.

"I'm glad to have the chance to speak to you alone, Miss Melville," he said at last. "Tell me, why are you going along with all this?"

"I'm not going along with all this. I'm trying to keep out of it."

"Then why didn't you just tell Mother that flat out? Why did you come here tonight?"

She couldn't tell him she was preparing the ground for his mother's demise. "I hadn't seen her for forty years—I wanted to catch up on old times."

He eyed her skeptically.

"And I was curious to meet you."

He smiled. It was an attractive smile. "Oh, and what do you think of me?"

"You're not what I expected."

"And what did you expect? More of a wimp?"

"Something like that," she admitted.

"I know it's hard for you to understand the way I've been acting—or not acting," he said. "Believe me, I have my reasons. But I can't tell anyone what they are, not even Audrey."

There was nothing she could say in reply to that, not even that she understood, because she didn't understand.

"But then I can't figure you out either. Mother said you were definitely going to join the board of trustees. Was she lying again?"

"Not exactly," Susan admitted. "I didn't tell her I would join the board. On the other hand, I didn't tell her I wouldn't."

"Why not?"

She shrugged. "Oh, like you, I have my reasons."

"I thought perhaps"—he hesitated—"she might be blackmailing you, too. It's an ugly little habit of hers, blackmail."

Too? So Andy had been right. The Begum did have something she was holding over her son's head. But then Andy was almost always right. It was an ugly little habit of his.

"Was it something you did as a child?" Serwar persisted. "But surely after all these years it must be long since forgotten, and probably it wasn't anything so terrible to begin with."

144

She smiled and shook her head.

"Believe me, I'm not trying to pry into your affairs. It just occurred to me that she might be trying to blackmail you because of that fellow you killed outside Rundle House. I'm sure you must have had a very good reason," he added hastily.

Oh, Lord, Susan thought, I seem to have been playing to a larger audience than I imagined. Should she pull out the stock phrase: I have absolutely no idea what you're talking about?

No, he deserved better than that. "Were you the one who saw me?"

"No, if it had been I, I'm afraid that, not knowing who you were, and not knowing who the—er—object of your attention was, I would have called the police."

"Yes, you would, wouldn't you," his mother said from the doorway. "Self-righteous little pig—prig—whatever. You could have gummed up the whole operation."

"Then I wish I had been there," Serwar said. "Even if it meant turning you in, Miss Melville. You do understand, don't you?"

"I'm glad you didn't see me," she said.

"The only one who saw you was an attaché from the Gandistani Mission who happened to be there on business. He's back in Gandistan now. You don't have to worry about him."

"I already told her that," Berry said, holding on to the back of a chair to steady herself. She seemed to have sobered up a little, but she was still by no means sober. "I always play fair."

He shook his head. "No, Mother, you never play fair."

"What I also told her was that I'd kill her if she didn't join the board. That was when she caved in."

"I didn't cave in. I merely said I'd think about it, and I'm still thinking."

"What was it with the girls of your generation?" Serwar asked. "Did they teach you to become killers in those exclusive private schools of yours?"

"You're a fine one to talk about exclusive private schools," his mother said. "You were tooted by tauters. Taught by tutors. What could be more exclusive than that?"

He laughed. "I suppose that did sound funny, coming from me. I must have got it from Audrey. She's against privilege."

"She's a Commie," Berry said. "A rose red Commie. 'The King and the Communist.' What a title for a romantic novel. Or how about 'the Sultan and the Socialist?' "

145

"Don't you think you'd better go to bed, Mother?"

"I'm not in the leasht sleepy. Maybe I'll kill Audrey, too," she said musingly. "Solve everything." She appeared to think. "Well, not everything, but a lot."

Susan looked at Serwar. He seemed unimpressed by the threat. "Go to bed, Mother. I told Jumaan and Azra they could take the rest of the evening off after dinner, so it's the Waldorf staff that are going to come clear away the dinner things. We don't want to run the risk of having any of them see you in that state. It's not the impiety I'm worried about," he explained to Susan, "it's the embarrassment."

XXII

"**I**'LL CALL YOU in the morning," Berry said, "an' we'll fish it up about Bloomingdale's."

"Do you think you'll feel up to shopping tomorrow?"

Berry looked indignant. "Shertainly. Why shouldn't I be?"

Well, if she wanted to go shopping—or shooting—with a hangover, far be it from Susan to dissuade her. At the same time, she couldn't just sit around waiting for Berry to call her. "I have an early morning appointment, so I might leave before you get up. Why don't we arrange when and where we're going to meet now?"

"Good idea. Shave a lot of trouble. Ten o'clock? No, maybe 'leven would be better, jus' in case I sleep late."

"Which of the front doors shall we meet by?"

Berry shook her head for a somewhat longer time than a simple negative required. "No, I hate waiting by doors. It makes me feel ekshpozhed. How about Intimate Attire—Intimashies—whatever they call it? You know, underwear. Tha'sh where we were heading when Lucy started carrying on."

"Mother, Aunt Lucy got sick. She couldn't help it."

"She could, too, if she put her mind to it." Berry gripped the chair so hard she canted to one side. Her son took her by the arm and righted her. "An' I wanna go to the Main Dish," Berry said. "Get glashes of my own. Drink whenever I like."

"Main Dish?" Serwar asked.

"They call the floor where they sell housewares and dishes something like that," Susan explained.

"Oh," he said.

"So you'll take a cab downtown," Berry crooned, "an' I'll take a cab uptown."

And, with any luck, Susan thought, I'll be in Bloomingdale's afore you.

"We'll meet on the third floor at 'leven. How does that sound to you? Or would you prefer to meet on the 'leventh floor at three?"

"The third floor at eleven will be fine," Susan said. "Bloomingdale's doesn't have eleven floors."

"That wouldn't sh-shtop me."

"But where shall we meet? The place is a maze."

"Why don't we meet by the eshkalators? I love eshkalators. We don't have 'em in Gandistan and very few lellelevators."

"And very few buildings more than two stories high," her son pointed out.

"That will all change. I have plans that will ashton-ashton-shurprise you." She pointed a finger at Susan. "The limou-limou-car will take you back now. That is, if you're going home. I don't want to rush you."

"I am going home, but really it isn't necessary to get the limousine out for me."

"It is neshesary. Gandistanis do not let their guests go home by themselves. There might be tigers. It'sh a jungle out there. S-sonny will make the arrangements. Nighty-night." She held out her cheek for her guest to kiss; then, with a valedictory hiccup, she staggered off in an aura of alcohol and sandalwood.

Serwar sighed. "She gets worse and worse, and there's nothing I can do. Anyhow, I'll drive you home myself. There are some things I want to say that I don't want anyone to hear."

"But surely we're private enough here."

"We'll be more private in a car. Just because Mother has gone to bed doesn't mean she'll stay there."

"I hope she'll feel well enough to go shopping tomorrow," Susan said, trying to sound concerned without sounding anxious.

"Mother has a pretty hard head. But I doubt that it will stop her from going shopping. I doubt that anything would stop her from going shopping."

And if it does, Susan thought, I'll just have to postpone her killing to another day. But I will be disappointed.

"I'LL CALL THE garage," he said. He left.

Susan was not happy at the prospect of being driven home by him. She knew that his blood alcohol level had to be way above the legal limit, even though it didn't show. The Rundle men had always been able to hold their liquor. Up to a point. And you never knew when that point had been passed. She visualized the headlines: POTENTATE AND PAINTER DIE IN FIERY CRASH. Or: "PAINTER AND POTENTATE DIE IN FIERY CRASH. Depending on which paper you read.

She could offer to drive, but she didn't know how he would take such a suggestion. Even American men hated having their sobriety questioned. She could propose that they both leave in the limousine; then he could come up to her apartment and they could talk there. But that would mean the limousine with the two turbaned men would be waiting downstairs all the while, attracting nosy neighbors like a lodestone.

Serwar was off telephoning for what seemed like a long time, although according to her watch it took only ten minutes. "The car's waiting. You didn't have a coat or anything, did you? All right, let's go."

Downstairs, a dark blue Mercedes was waiting for them. Also waiting was the silver stretch limousine, complete with the two turbaned men. There was a short discussion in Gandistani, accompanied by a pantomime so expressive that Susan had no trouble understanding what they were saying. The two turbans were telling the king his mother wouldn't like him to be chauffeuring their guest himself, to which he was replying, "Who's the king here, anyway?"

Finally they bowed, got into the limousine, and drove off.

"They'll follow us, of course," he said, as he and Susan got into the Mercedes, "but I'm accustomed to being followed. Usually less obtrusively, but they're stuck with the limo. If they stop to get another car, they'll lose us. Not that we'd be alone even if they did lose us," he added, as the car swung out into Park Avenue. "You'll notice that

149

there'll be another car behind the limo and maybe another car after that."

"I noticed when I was driving with your mother that there did seem to be some cars following us. Who were they?"

He shrugged. "Local enforcement agencies, perhaps, anxious to protect us or to see what Mother and I are up to. Possibly some Gandistani organization, for the same reason."

"The—er—board of trustees?" Susan ventured.

"The Mafiosi, you mean?" He laughed. "Maybe they'd follow Mother; I doubt that they'd follow me. They wouldn't think I was worth following."

There was a bitter note in his voice. Susan could not sympathize. She did not feel that the fact that the Mafia did not consider you worth following was an occasion for bitterness.

SERWAR MADE A right turn and headed east. Stopping the car next to a little park overlooking the East River Drive, he opened the door for her. "Let's get out here. We can't talk in the car. Someone might have bugged it—planted a listening device."

"I know what 'bugged' means," Susan said.

The park was very dark and quiet. At first it seemed empty. Then she could make out the shadowy forms of bodies stretched out on the benches, perhaps sleeping, perhaps not. "Do you think it's entirely safe here?" she asked. "Some of those homeless people can be dangerous."

"Audrey says we shouldn't call them homeless," he observed. " 'Residentially disadvantaged' is what we're supposed to say."

Susan had some very unkind thoughts about Audrey. "Whatever you call them, it doesn't make them less dangerous."

"No, I should say it would probably make them more dangerous. At least if they heard it," he added with a smile. He seemed to know what was passing through her mind. "Audrey does get a little excessive in her zeal. But you must agree that it's a fault on the right side."

Susan didn't agree at all. She changed the subject. "Does Gandistan have a lot of homeless people?"

"No, we're too small and poor to be able to afford such luxuries."

He took her arm, and urged her toward the park. "There's no need to worry about this lot. Look, Ali and Samir are keeping an eye on us."

He pointed with his free hand. Half a block away she could see the

150

limousine parked in the shadows, glimmering like a ghostly chariot. "They're licensed bodyguards, so they're armed," he told her.

He looked at her with a faint smile. "And, come to think of it, I wouldn't be surprised to discover you were carrying a gun, too."

She gave the deprecating murmur that had, in the past, usually stood her in good stead when the conversation took an awkward turn.

"Mother said it was quite customary for a woman in New York to carry a gun when she's going to a neighborhood like the one Rundle House is in, but Audrey goes into even rougher neighborhoods in the course of her work, and she never carries a gun."

"Then Audrey's braver than I am," Susan said, mentally crossing her fingers. A dismaying thought struck her. "You didn't tell Audrey about that Lord man . . . ?"

"Of course not. She wouldn't understand. What's more, she wouldn't believe me. She thinks a lot of you."

Under the circumstances, Susan was not unduly gratified by the compliment. I hope she isn't under the impression that I'm politically correct, she thought.

SERWAR AND SUSAN leaned over the rail and looked at the river down below. It was a beautiful spring night. The air was soft and warm and a faint breeze rippled the reflection of the moon in the water. You could hardly smell the garbage floating past. It was very quiet except for the occasional faraway scream across the river, from Queens.

For a moment Susan wished it had been someone other than Serwar standing beside her. Not that he wasn't an attractive young man, but he was the son of her childhood friend (loosely speaking). He had been gracious enough not to call her "Aunt Susan" at his Mother's behest, but, if she asked him not to call her Miss Melville, then Aunt Susan was what he probably would call her. Hadn't he threatened as much? How could she have romantic ideas about anyone who called her Aunt Susan?

If only it could have been Gil Frias standing beside her, or possibly that nice young artist who had been so attentive to her at the Von Schwabes' dinner party the week before last. But Gil was having trouble in his own country with a group of dissidents so incoherent in their manifestos that no one, including, many felt, the dissidents themselves, was sure whether they belonged to the radical right or the radical left. As for the young artist, she couldn't remember his name, and, if he remembered hers, she told herself, it would be only because it was a celebrated one.

However, there were advantages to celebrity. After she had taken care of Berry tomorrow, she would, if she were still in a position to do so, call Mimi von Schwabe and see if she could weasel the young man's name out of her without Mimi's realizing what her friend was up to. Mimi tended to be very protective of her protégés.

Peter . . . ? Did Susan wish he were standing beside her? She would be glad to see him again, of course, but it was a long time since she had thought of him in connection with romance. If he were there now, they would probably be discussing the foundation's expenses, which had been increasingly over budget of late. She wondered whether he ever spoke to Dr. Froehlich about romance? She wondered again whether Dr. Froehlich had gone down to South America with the expedition? Dr. Froehlich had been asked to resign from the Foundation back in January, but the expedition had not been Foundation-sponsored.

She really must call that young man from the foundation. Towers, that was his name, Ralph Towers, to ask if he'd heard anything from Peter. And, while she was talking to him, she might ask casually what Dr. Froehlich was doing now.

"AUDREY SAID SHE was planning to get in touch with you," Serwar said.

"Audrey? With me? I hope she doesn't want me to serve on a committee because I'm already in over my head . . ."

"Nothing like that. I think she wants to talk about our situation. Hers and mine, I mean. She can't talk to anyone she knows. It's not that her friends don't know about her and me; it was no secret while I was going to school here. But she didn't know about the Rundle connection then. Now that she's met Mother and does know, I've asked her not to tell anyone."

"And, since I already do know, she feels she can talk to me?"

He nodded.

"Did Audrey meet your mother here or in Gandistan?"

"Here. I've been here a few times since I left school. I arrived much less conspicuously since these weren't state visits, which getting an honorary degree at Harvard is, more or less. And once all three of us got together in Paris."

"Has Audrey ever been to Gandistan?"

He shook his head. "No, Mother invited her to come for a visit, but I advised against it. You never know what Mother might do."

Susan could imagine. "Audrey sounds like a determined young lady. Supposing she decided to go, anyway."

He smiled. "Gandistan doesn't exactly encourage tourism. And I've given instructions that if Audrey applies for a visa she isn't to get one."

SUSAN AND SERWAR watched the water for a few minutes without speaking. A sightseeing boat glided past. Apparently some kind of party was being held on board because suddenly the comparative peace of the night was broken by raucous laughter and the sound of what passed for music in these degenerate days.

Several of the recumbent figures on the benches stirred restlessly. One sat up and waved his fist, before subsiding into his previous position.

"I know it sounds crazy," Serwar said, "but I think you should watch out for Mother. Sometimes I get the feeling that she doesn't like you as much as she says she does."

"Sometimes I get the same feeling, especially when she threatened to kill me if I didn't became a member of the board of trustees."

"Oh, I'm sure she was only joking about that. The board of trustees can't be that important, even to her." But he spoke the words without conviction.

My joining the board of trustees isn't that important, Susan realized. It's my *not* joining that's important. She wants an excuse to kill me, something that would make sense to her twisted mind—or maybe something that would mean the Bat would be less upset if I were dead (although I don't suppose she'd let him know she was my killer, just to be on the safe side). She invited me to go shopping with her at Bloomingdale's because she realized as soon as she saw it that it was the perfect place in which to shoot me. She doesn't know I thought it would be the perfect place to shoot her. Or does she?

"I'M SURPRISED AUDREY hasn't called you yet," Serwar said. "When I told her yesterday that you were going to have dinner tonight with Mother and me, she said she was going to call you up before you left. And, when Audrey says she's going do so something, she always does it."

153

"Maybe she did call and Michelle forgot to tell me. Michelle's my housekeeper," she explained. "Taking messages is not one of her strong points. Of course, I'd be happy to talk to Audrey, but I don't see what good I could do. From what you say, it isn't your mother who's standing in the way of your marriage, it's Audrey herself."

"Oh, you mean because she won't convert? That's the official story. The truth is that Audrey's perfectly willing to embrace Islam. She says all religions are equal in the sight of God. Or the gods, depending. As long as you lead a"—he looked embarrassed; after all, he had been to Harvard—"moral life."

"Sort of the Abou Ben Adhem approach?"

Serwar looked defiant. "Audrey may not be perfect, but I love her."

Susan wondered if she were expected to say something supportive, like "Good for you!" She didn't. "Maybe she changed her mind about calling me—" she began. Then she remembered Michelle's laundry list. Sheets could have been Skeat. And, yes, pillowcases might be Pilokis, the contractor. And towels? Towers, of course. When she got back home, she would call Ralph Towers right away. Pilokis she would leave to Jill. And Audrey? Susan would wait and see what the morrow would bring.

"The truth of the matter is," Serwar said, "Audrey says she won't marry me unless I get rid of Mother."

Susan was startled. There seemed to be more to Audrey than she had imagined. But she was disappointed in Serwar. Getting rid of one's enemies was one thing, but even the ancient Greeks, who were by no means squeamish, had frowned at matricide. And Serwar seemed like such a nice boy, too.

She felt relieved when he went on, "Audrey wants me to pension Mother off and exile her from Gandistan. It isn't as if she would be alone in a strange land. She was born here and she has family here. So it shouldn't be a real hardship, especially as Mother kept telling Audrey how she was never happy in Gandistan. Actually, I think she was very happy there, particularly after my father became senile and she took over, which wasn't as long after their marriage as she would have people think, because otherwise it would make her responsible for a lot of things even she doesn't want to be held responsible for."

"Well, why don't you do that? Pension your mother off, I mean. It sounds to me like the ideal solution to your problems. And, if you do it fast enough, you'd still have a chance of stopping the—ah—Rundle House gang from taking over your country. I gather the whole thing is still in the planning stage, that they haven't established a presence there."

He nodded. "No, none of the bigwigs have ever even been there. However, Mother won't take kindly to the idea of being pensioned off."

"But what can she do if you put your foot down? After all, you're the king."

There was a very long pause. "Not really," he said.

XXIII

FOR A MOMENT she thought she'd misunderstood him. Then, from the expression on his face, she saw she had not. "You mean you're not Berry's son? Or your father's son?" Hanky-panky in the harem; that would explain a lot.

"Oh, I'm her son, all right. And I'm the sultan's son, too. I'm legitimate here in the United States, but not in Gandistan. You see, Mother never did convert to Islam. She and my father were married outside Gandistan, in an Episcopalian ceremony, she tells me. Her father, my grandfather, insisted on it. He said Rundles always had Episcopalian weddings, no matter whom they married."

"I did wonder about that," Susan said, "but she told me your grandfather didn't mind her converting to Islam. Of course, she would have had to say that, wouldn't she, if she didn't want me to know the truth?"

Serwar nodded glumly.

"What I can't understand is why, under those circumstances, your father gave in and married her at all?"

"I suppose he was crazy to have her. His mind must have been going even then."

Children never seemed to realize, Susan thought ruefully, that their parents had once been comely and desirable.

"And they were outside Gandistan when they got married, so he couldn't just have taken her by force, the way he could have at home. Anyhow, according to Islamic law, I'm illegitimate. So now you know why she can make me do anything she wants—almost anything, anyhow."

After a pause, he said, "I've never told anyone about this before, not even Audrey, and I'm sure Mother's never told anyone; she'd probably have signed her own death warrant if she had. But I don't know what to do, and I've got to do something. Before, when Mother was simply running Gandistan, I could say to myself: Well, things aren't any worse than they were before. I can just let them go on the way they are until—well—it isn't that I want anything to happen to Mother, of course, but she isn't a young woman . . ." His voice trailed off, as he met Susan's eye.

"She isn't all that old," Susan said coldly. "She could last for years."

He looked abashed. "Oh, I am sorry, Miss Melville. I didn't think. But you seem so much younger than Mother. Probably because you keep yourself in such good shape."

He went off on a tactful tangent. "When Audrey becomes queen—if she becomes queen, I should say—she's planning to institute a system of universal physical education, she says. Make Gandistan the fittest nation in the world."

Susan had begun to suspect it before; now she was sure of it. Audrey was not the right girl for Serwar. There must be someone I know who would make him a more suitable wife, she thought, and she ran through all the princesses of her acquaintance in her mind. None of them seemed right.

"BUT HOW CAN your mother get away with it?" Susan asked. "I know you said she never told anyone, but there must be other people who know you're not exactly legitimate."

He shook his head. "There's no one who could possibly know. No one who's alive, anyway. Mother's never had any confidants. And, as I've said she was married outside of Gandistan—where, I don't know;

she would never tell me. Maybe there are records, but nobody would know where to look for them."

"You said no one who's alive," she said. "You mean your grandfather, I suppose."

"At the time she was married, I think the current prime minister might have known, too, but he died soon after. Rumor said he was poisoned, but they always say that whenever anyone dies of natural causes in Gandistan. Besides, even if he was poisoned, he had lots of enemies before she ever got there. Prime ministers always do. It goes with the job."

"Your mother said something about your step-brothers' having killed him."

"That was his successor. I was too young to remember exactly what did happen to him. And the prime minister I do remember was openly beheaded; no mystery there. Since then there hasn't been a prime minister. And"—he laughed a little—"no great rush of applicants for the position."

Susan was not interested in Gandistani's politics. "If your mother is the only one who can prove you're not legitimate, I don't see why it should worry you."

"Don't you see? That's what she's blackmailing me with. If I don't go along with what she wants, she says, she'll tell everyone I have no claim to the throne."

Susan didn't see. She didn't see at all. "But if you lose your power, she'll lose her power. Why don't you call her bluff? Tell her to publish and be damned."

"It's more like publish and perish. You don't know Mother. Or, rather, you do know Mother. You should know she'd cut off her nose to spite her face any day."

"But she'd have to be crazy to—" Susan broke off in mid-sentence. Berry *was* crazy.

"There wouldn't be any financial incentive for her to keep her mouth shut either," he continued. "She's been siphoning money from the treasury over the years, so I know she has a healthy account tucked away in a bank in some other country—which is one of the reasons Gandistan is so poor. Any pension I could afford to give her would be ridiculous. If she told the people of Gandistan the truth about me, she'd be quite comfortably off, provided she got away in time, and she'd be sure to do that. And, unless she gave me a chance to do the same thing, I'd be dead."

158

"They wouldn't just kick you out?"

"No, they wouldn't." He ran his hand through his thick, dark hair. "The worst part of it is that I'm not sure the whole thing isn't a ploy of Mother's to get me to do what she wants, and she converted to Islam and married my father in a perfectly legal Muslim ceremony."

"DOES IT MEAN so much to you to be king?" Susan asked.

"Are you suggesting that I just walk out while I'm here in this country, marry Audrey, settle down here, and get a job?"

"Well, yes, more or less."

He sighed, and leaned with his back to the rail. "Don't think I haven't thought about it. I wouldn't have any trouble getting a job; there's always a modest demand in this country for ex-kings. I could be a car salesman, professor, lobbyist, lots of things. And, even if I couldn't find a job, I wouldn't starve. I'm entitled to my share of the Rundle trust."

"I'm sure Audrey would be pleased," Susan said.

She was by no means sure that this would be true and neither, it seemed, was Serwar. "I'm afraid she might be disappointed. She's set her heart on being queen and establishing a new order, which is difficult when you're trying to bring in democracy, because people don't always want a new order. But Audrey wouldn't want me to be king if she knew I wasn't legally entitled to the throne," he finished confidently.

"Don't you think the best thing for you to do would be simply to abdicate while you're here? You wouldn't even have to say that you think you might be illegitimate. Just do a reprise of Edward VIII."

It was a while before his answer came. "I suppose this is hard for you to believe, Miss Melville, but my roots are in Gandistan. I love my country. If I thought it would be good for Gandistan, I'd abdicate like a shot and live in exile for the rest of my life. But, if I do, my cousin Abdul would become king. He's next in line. If something should happen to me."

"Abdul is the one whom the Mafia—or was it your Mother?—picked to head their—er—operations?"

He nodded. "He's the largest opium grower in Gandistan, but that's not enough for him; he wants to make it internationally, and he doesn't care how he does it."

"He doesn't sound like a nice man."

"He isn't, but he isn't nearly as bad as my cousin Karim, who's the

159

second largest poppy grower. Karim also could assert a claim to the throne if something should happen to me. If he does, there could be a bloody civil war."

"Don't you have any nice relatives?"

"Princes don't stay in power by being nice," he observed. "Whichever of them succeeds in the end, Gandistan will be turned into a major international drug processing center, just the way they've planned it, only without Mother, and they don't really need Mother."

"So you're the only one who could save your country?"

He winced. "I know it sounds conceited, but it's true. If I become king in fact as well as name I can put an end to their plans before they start. As it stands now, the army would be loyal to me. But once the Mafia have established themselves and their people in the country it would be too late."

It was clear now why Andy wanted to get rid of Berry, though why the people in his own agency didn't handle the matter themselves, now that she was in the country and an easy target, was beyond Susan. Perhaps they always subcontracted assassinations so they could claim that their hands were clean. She hated to play into their hands by disposing of Berry, but she would be doing it for her own sake, and perhaps for King Serwar's, but not for theirs. And she could always console herself with the knowledge that this way she was saving the taxpayers money. They wouldn't even have to pay for the bullet.

"I SUPPOSE THE first thing you'd do if you got your power is to destroy the opium fields," she suggested.

He looked startled. "I couldn't do that. The economy would collapse. Opium is our major industry as well as our only cash crop."

"How do you think Audrey would feel about your continuing to grow opium?"

He looked thoughtful. "We've never discussed it," he said.

I'll bet you haven't, Susan thought.

"But that's a bridge I'll cross when I come to it. Right now the thing to do is put a crimp in Mother's plans. I don't suppose you have any ideas?"

None that I'm going to divulge to you, she thought. "Maybe she could be declared *non compos mentis* as Berengaria Rundle while she's here. There's a very nice place where she could stay. I believe there are several members of your family living there already. But, of course, she can claim Gandistani citizenship. All they'd be able to do is deport her."

"And in Gandistan she's as sane as any member of the royal family ever has been," he said sadly.

XXIV

SUDDENLY THERE CAME a screech. A man had leaped up, either from a bench or out of the bushes, and was waving a knife at the two Gandistani attendants. "Alien invaders!" he shrieked. "Come to take over the earth. Begone! Take your spaceship and return to the stars, or I'll rip out your gizzards!"

His words made a crazy kind of sense. The stretch limousine looked as much like a spaceship as it did a regular car. In the moonlight, the two turbans, with a stretch of the imagination, could resemble space helmets. But neither Ali nor Samir looked like birds, and only birds, Susan believed, had gizzards. Oh, well, one couldn't expect biological accuracy from a madman.

One of the two bodyguards drew a gun. "Don't shoot, Ali!" Serwar cried. "He's crazy. He doesn't know what he's doing."

Ali said something in his own language. He didn't lower his gun. Probably in Gandistan Serwar's words wouldn't make a whole lot of sense. Like most backward peoples, the Gandistanis would think, in their simplicity, that the only way to deal with a homicidal maniac was to kill him before he started carving up the community

Serwar ran toward the man who was brandishing the knife. The man continued to advance. As he came into the pool of light cast by a street lamp, Susan saw him more clearly. He didn't look like a homeless person. His clothing, though casual, seemed to hail from Ralph Lauren rather than Canal Street. Probably he shopped at one of the better thrift shops. Susan had gotten some nice buys there in her preaffluent days, she recalled.

Before Serwar could reach the maniac, two men in business suits came up, one on either side of him. Each gripped him by an arm. The knife clattered to the ground.

"Police officers," one of the business-suited men said, showing a badge. The other one said nothing. He was Andrew Mackay. He carefully did not look in her direction. Let him tell me that he has no official connection with the government after this, she thought, keeping her own face a studied blank.

A police car rolled up. Two uniformed policemen emerged and took the man into custody. He didn't resist while they handcuffed them; in fact, he seemed to recognize them as old acquaintances. "Hello, Joe," he said. "Hello, Bert. It's been a while since I've seen you. You're looking good."

"You're looking pretty good yourself," one of the policemen replied.

SEVERAL CARS DROVE past in almost ceremonial procession, each with two men (or, in one case, a man and a woman) in it, all aggressively minding their own business. These, too, must have been watching them, Susan gathered. Such a lot of attention devoted to one minor monarch and one important but innocuous artist. Probably some of the people in some of the cars had been watching other people in the other cars.

"We've had trouble with this gentleman before," Bert or Joe explained. She wasn't sure whether he was addressing Serwar and herself or Andy and his companion, but, as the only unofficial representative of the American people present, she took it upon herself to reply.

"So sad about the homeless. If only they had access to proper psychiatric treatment . . ."

"Oh, Mr. Frobisher's not homeless."

Mr. Frobisher bowed, seeming to take this as an introduction. Susan, not to be outdone in courtesy, gave him a gracious inclination of her head.

"And he's under constant psychiatric care. He's a retired stockbroker. Lives on Beekman Place. Overdosed on 'Star Trek' when he was young, or so they say. Every now and then when the moon's full he gets away from his attendants and comes out here to watch for invaders from space. First time I've seen him with a weapon, though."

"First time I ever caught any invaders," Mr. Frobisher pointed out. "Of course, if I'd known you were watching, I would never have taken it on myself to repel them. I have the utmost faith in New York's finest, no matter what people say."

"So nice to have met you," he called to Susan, as he was stuffed into the police car. "You know all about me. Perhaps we could do lunch one of these days, and you can tell me all about yourself."

The police car departed, Andy and his associate vanished into the shadows. Ali and Samir got back into the limousine. All was as before. "I feel as though I'd been part of a show," Susan said.

"In a way, I suppose, you have. Well, now I've got my secret off my chest, you know what? I don't feel any better. In fact, I feel worse."

"I'm sorry I couldn't have been of more help," Susan said.

"No need to blame yourself. Probably there's no one who could help me. Maybe you're right. Maybe abdication is the only answer. If I can't save my people, at least I can save myself. There are worse things than exile, I suppose."

"Don't be in a hurry to abdicate. Maybe we can think of something less drastic." Or more drastic, she thought; only he wasn't to know that.

"IT'S GETTING LATE. I think I'd better drive you home."

Both of them were silent on the way back. He escorted her to her front door and bade her good night. The neighbors who hung out in the lobby at all hours paid no attention. If only they knew he was a king, Susan thought, they would be all over him.

When she got upstairs, she looked up Ralph Towers' number and called him. Only an answering machine responded. She left a message, then started to check her tape to see if anyone else had tried to reach her.

Before she could finish, the phone rang. "Susie! 'Bout time you got home. I tried to reach you before, but a machine answered. I don't talk to no machines."

"Why, Mr. Battaglia—"

"Carlo."

"Why, Carlo, how—how nice to hear from you. I was planning to write you and thank you for the beautiful flowers."

"Glad you liked 'em," he said. "And you don't hafta write. That's too formal for old friends like us. So, tell me, how'd the dinner with Queenie go? Did she tell ya about the great things we're gonna do for Rundle House? Did she make you see you gotta be a member of the board of trusties? We need ya, Susie, we need ya."

How did he know about her dinner with Berry? Had Berry told him about it? Or had he been having either Berry or Susan herself watched? More likely Berry. For which she could hardly blame him. If she'd been about to go into a business venture with Berry Rundle, she would watch her like a hawk.

"We didn't talk about Rundle House at all. We were too busy reminiscing about old times. And this was the first time I'd met her son."

"Yeah, Serwar, Sonny, whatever his name is. Snotty kid. Although, of course, bein' a king, I guess he can't help bein' snotty."

"He seems to me like a pleasant, unaffected young man."

"Well, people like that—kings, princes, even dooks, I shunt be surprised—are brought up not to show their feelin's, so you can't expect him to be affectionate. His mom said somethin' about him wantin' to marry an American girl. And not a society girl, either. You'd think he'd marry a princess, somebody like that, keep the royal blood blue."

"Times have changed. Look at the British royal family."

"Yeah, just look at 'em."

It had been narrow-minded of her, Susan thought, to restrict her attention to princesses in connection with Serwar's prospective bride. There were plenty of red-blooded American girls who might make him a good wife. Amy Patterson's youngest, whatever her name was. And didn't Mimi have some nieces who might be eligible? She would have to look into them.

"WELL, I DIN'T call ya to gossip about the love life of royal folks; I called to ast if you could have dinner with me tomorrow night."

She didn't want to accept any invitations until she had completed her task at Bloomingdale's. Even if all turned out well, she wasn't sure he wanted to have dinner with Carlo Battaglia on the evening of the day he lost a business associate. In fact, she wasn't sure she wanted to have

dinner with Carlo Battaglia at all. It wasn't that she was image conscious, but it wouldn't look well for a serious artist to be seen having
dinner with a notorious gangster, even if she had Jill spread it around
that he was thinking of starting an art collection.

"I'm afraid I'm not free tomorrow night," she said, wondering
whether declining a dinner invitation from a Mafia don was the mob
equivalent of *lèse-majesté*.

"What about Friday?"

She couldn't keep putting him off. "Friday will be fine," she said.
Would he take her to Federigo's Fish House? At least Federigo's was
not likely to attract gossip columnists.

"Good. I'll make reservations in some classy place. You got any pref-
erences? Four Seasons? Lutèce? Palm? You name it."

She couldn't say she would prefer Federigo's Fish House. "They're
all fine with me." She tried to console herself with the thought that it
wasn't likely that he'd be able to get reservations at a "classy place" on
such short notice. On the other hand, maybe *he* could.

"Then I'll pick ya up at—say—seven?"

"I'll be looking forward to it," she said, trying not to strangle on the
words.

He started to bid her good night; then interrupted himself. "Oh, by
the way, when're ya gonna see Queenie again?"

"I'm going to see her tomorrow."

"You two havin' lunch?"

"We're going shopping at Bloomingdale's. I suppose we will have
lunch afterward." Why was he quizzing her like this?

"Bloomingdale's," he repeated. "Fine store, fine store. My late wife,
God rest her soul, would never shop anywhere else. Always kept astin'
me to go there with her, but I never had the time."

He sighed, as if the late Mrs. Battaglia would be alive today if he had
agreed to accompany her to Bloomingdale's. "Did Queenie tell you I'm
thinkin' of maybe buyin' the place? I meantersay if the price is right."

"She did say something about it."

"Mind ya don't say nuttin' about it to nobody," he cautioned her.
"Once people know you're interested, the price goes up."

"I wouldn't think of it."

" 'Course not. But it never hurts to make sure. Well, I'll be countin'
the minutes till Friday. Sweet dreams, Susie, and I hope I'm in 'em."

He was, but not in any way he would have appreciated.

XXV

T HE NEXT MORNING Susan got up and searched through her wardrobe for an outfit suitable for stalking a human quarry through a department store. A tweed suit would seem most fitting and would probably be a fashion editor's selection, but the sleeves of a tailored jacket would almost certainly be a hindrance, unless it had been specially designed for shooting. In the end, she opted for a short-sleeved slate blue linen dress with a matching long-sleeved jacket which she would later take off and carry draped over her arm to conceal her gun until such time as she was ready to use it. She hoped she wouldn't be forced to shoot through the jacket. The ensemble was a favorite of hers. She'd been told that it matched her eyes.

She loaded her best Beretta and put it into the handbag she had bought at Bloomingdale's the day before—only right that a Bloomingdale's kill should be accessorized with a Bloomingdale's bag. Did Bloomingdale's sell guns? To use a Bloomingdale's gun would add to the symmetry of the occasion, but it was too late to do anything about that now.

She didn't feel hungry; however, she knew it would be a mistake to go on a hunting expedition on an empty stomach, so she forced herself to swallow a cup of coffee and eat a slightly stale croissant, which was all she could find in the kitchen.

Michelle arrived as she was finishing the croissant. "I was savin' that for myself," she complained.

"You can buy some more when you go shopping this morning," Susan said as she rose, "along with whatever else we need—which is practically everything. I've made you a list, but that's just for starters. Feel free to add to it if I've left out anything."

"Don't look like you lef' nothin' out," Michelle said, looking at the lengthy screed her employer had prepared. "Folks who run the supermarket are gonna be eatin' high off the hog for a long time after an order like this'un. Does this mean you're gonna be back for lunch?"

"I'm not sure."

"I wish you'd make up your mind. How can I make any plans if you don't make any plans?"

Susan counted to five. "Just plan to go shopping this morning so there'll be food in the house."

Michelle sighed. "Okay, okay. You're the boss."

As if there had been any doubt about it, Susan thought. She really must do something about Michelle. But there was time for that. Which is what I always keep telling myself, she thought.

"Whaddya want me to say if somebody calls? I 'spose you want me to lie for you again?"

"Just tell them the truth, that I'm out and you don't know where I am or when I'll be coming back."

"—'Sposin' that Mr. Towels starts callin' again? He was mighty anxious to reach you yestiddy. Lessen you got to talk to him las' evenin' . . . ?"

It was none of Michelle's business, but Susan didn't want her to think her employer had neglected any of the normal obligations of courtesy. "I did call him, but he wasn't in, so I left a message on his machine."

"Great. Now he's gonna call and drag me away from my work. How can you expeck me to get any work done if I hafta keep answerin' the phone?"

"I've told you over and over to leave the answering machine on. Then you won't have to answer any calls. In fact, I would prefer—"

"But some of the calls might be for me," Michelle objected. "I wooden wanna miss any of my calls. By the way, I meant to tell you.

Mr. Pillowcase said he insisted on talkin' to you personably; said he'd rather deal with Tilly the Hon than that there Miz Turkey."

Susan had planned to call Ralph Towers that morning, but she didn't want anything to distract her for her immediate project. Besides, she wanted to get to Bloomingdale's at least an hour before her appointment, so she could spy out the lay of the store, and it was almost ten o'clock now.

"I'll call Mr. Towers again from outside," she said, picking up her bag and gloves. "As for Mr. Pilokis, if he calls again, tell him he's going to have to deal with Miss Turkel. That's what I pay both of them for."

"What about Tilly the Hon?"

"Tilly . . . ? Oh, he'll have to take his chances."

"He! I thought he was a she!"

"You learn something new every day," Susan told her.

When she got to the lobby, Susan asked the doorman to hail her a cab. Hailing a cab was easy. Not so getting one. "Always a shortage of cabs at this hour," the doorman apologized as cab after cab sailed past with its light off. "People going to work, stuff like that."

He made it sound as if it were all part of some kind of plot. Perhaps it was, Susan thought. Why should everybody go to work at the same time or approximately the same time? It made sense in the dark ages but, now that artificial illumination had been invented, how much more efficiently the city's resources could be utilized—how much safer the city would be—if working hours were extended around the clock.

SHE COULD ALWAYS make the journey downtown on foot. Bloomingdale's was less than thirty blocks away—a mile and a half—no great distance for someone who lived in Manhattan, where feet were the only reliable method of transport. Under normal circumstances, she would have walked to the store and enjoyed it. But it would take her at least twenty minutes to get there, what with stopping for traffic lights and circling to avoid street solicitors. She couldn't afford to spend twenty minutes.

An unoccupied taxi appeared. With a cry of triumph, the doorman flung himself in front of it, at considerable risk to life and limb, but desperate measures were needed. A bankerly type was hailing that same cab from across the street, and bankers would stop at nothing to achieve their ends, especially now that chivalry had long since died in financial circles.

Susan rewarded the doorman with appropriate lavishness and got

169

inside the cab, twisting herself so she could look out of the rear window as she rode. Was anyone following her? Not that she could see, but a skillful tail would probably be able to conceal himself from her nonprofessional eye. No reason why anyone should follow her, she assured herself. It had been the king and the queen who were being followed on the previous days.

She arrived at Bloomingdale's. There was a demonstration going on outside for or against something or other. Ignoring the demonstrators, she entered the store, and, after evading the ladies who lurked in the aisles poised to spray shoppers with the latest scent, she got into an elevator. A young man who had obviously been less lucky in dodging the spritzers squeezed in through the doors just before they closed, filling the elevator with oppressive aromas.

Even though this was the classic behavior of a follower, at least in the movies, she might not have paid any attention to him had his face not been somehow familiar. Where had she seen him before? Not an acquaintance or the son of an acquaintance; his tailoring was too sharp for a member of her own circle.

There was a leather case slung over his shoulder—a squat case, too large to contain binoculars, and the wrong shape. A camera? No opening for a lens. A tape recorder, perhaps, or a radio. If she figured out what it was, perhaps she could figure out who he was.

She gave him a half smile in case he turned out to be someone she had encountered without noticing, like a delivery man or a supermarket clerk. He avoided her eye in a manner that was so furtive it increased her suspicions. So, instead of getting off at "Intimacies" on the third floor, she continued up to the fourth, where, according to the store directory, a ladies' room might be found.

On the fourth floor the store seemed as she had noticed before, to have departed from the traditional concept of aisle and counter almost entirely. Almost everything seemed to be arranged in clusters and boutiques, so that it was impossible to proceed on one's way in a straight line. As she zigged and zagged her way through to the rear of the store where, a map on the wall indicated, the ladies' room lay, she kept catching glimpses of the young man behind her in one of the many mirrors set all over at such angles that often the shopper found herself (or himself) walking into a reflection instead of his (or her) intended destination. Music kept playing, not loudly but insistently, while banks of television screens showed what she feared must be the latest fashions.

She went into the ladies' room. Let him try to follow me in here, she thought! However, her victory was only a moral one—and a transient one at that. There was no other exit, at least not for shoppers. There might have been some secret means of egress known only to store employees, but a fat lot of good that would do her.

She spent several minutes in the seclusion of a cubicle, practicing the art of taking off her jacket and draping it gracefully over her right arm, while, at the same time, she held her gun in her hand. She put the gun back in her handbag, since—she checked her watch—there were still twenty-nine minutes to go before her rendezvous with Berry; and she didn't want to run the risk of dropping the weapon absent-mindedly, in case she should happen to come across a really good buy. Putting the gun back, however, she was soon to find out, was a grave mistake.

WHEN SHE CAME out of the ladies' room, the young man was not only standing outside, he had extracted a portable telephone from the case he carried—so that mystery was solved—and was talking into it. "But I can't follow her into the ladies' room, Uncle Carlo—" he was saying, when he caught her eye and broke off. His face flushed a bright red. Squawking noises came from the instrument.

Another mystery solved. She recognized him now. "You're Nicky— whatever your last name is. Mr. Battaglia's nephew."

"Lady, I don't know what you're talking about," he said without conviction.

"If you don't stop following me, I shall complain to the management. Or I might not need to. There are store detectives all over the place."

Which was probably true. She'd better watch her own step.

The young man turned even brighter red. "I was not following you," he said. "I—"

"It's my belief you're some kind of pervert. Loitering outside the ladies' room with a cellular phone and making suggestive remarks as people come out." Her voice was not loud, but clear and carrying.

"He must be sick," a young woman dressed in the height of fashionable bad taste said to her similarly attired companion as they emerged from the ladies' room. "Imagine making suggestive remarks to *her*!"

Both of them giggled. Nicky's face was like a sunset. He tried to stuff the phone back in its case. "I was not making suggestive remarks to her," he gulped. "Or anybody. I—I was just standing here, minding my own business. I—I—"

171

And he turned and fled, plunging into a rack of garments which collapsed, taking him down with them in a tangle of wildly patterned organzas from which, Susan thought with satisfaction, he would not be able to extricate himself in time to avoid the stern-looking young man, obviously a Bloomingdale employee, bearing down on him.

The two young women burst into girlish laughter. Susan could almost feel sorry for the unfortunate Nicky.

What was Nicky doing in the store? Clearly he had been dispatched by his uncle to keep an eye on her. But why? Was the Bat aware of Berry's plan to terminate Susan? Even less likely, did he suspect Susan's plans to terminate Berry? No, it was impossible that he could have known what was in Susan's mind, only minimally less likely that Berry would have confided her intentions to him. What did it matter? She had twenty-five minutes left to check out the third floor, pick her vantage point, and get out her gun, so she had better get cracking.

SHE REACHED THE top of the escalator leading down to the third floor. There seemed to be some sort of disturbance at the bottom. A stout lady dressed in a purple silk suit topped by a sable stole and a floppy cream-colored hat was hitting a young man over the head with a large stiff leather hand bag. "Get away from me, you sex fiend!" she was shrieking.

The young man was whimpering. Could Nicky have gotten downstairs that quickly? No, this was another young man who looked very much like Nicky, and dressed very much like him, even to the leather case banging against his side and which, Susan presumed, held another cellular telephone.

Shoppers smiled as they passed, clearly thinking that this was a piece of performance art devised by Bloomingdale's in its constant effort to keep the tourists entertained. Under other circumstances, Susan would have thought the same.

As the escalator started moving downward, bearing Susan inexorably toward "Intimacies," the lady in purple gave the young man's head a final thump. He ran off, howling.

The stout lady looked up and met Susan's eyes. Susan should have realized that, if she planned to come early, the same idea might have occurred to Berry. Hadn't Berry herself pointed out that they thought the same way? A result of their upbringing, of course, rather than any similarities of character, Susan assured herself.

172

For the first time a dreadful thought occurred to her. Her father had taught her to shoot. Her father had also taught Berry to shoot. Although she had denied it before—to Berry, to herself—was it possible that Berry was as good as a shot as Susan was? Was it possible that Berry was an even better shot than Susan?

XXVI

WHETHER SHE WAS as good a shot as Susan or not, she certainly had the drop on her. Susan's gun was still in her handbag. Berry's gun—it had a jewelled handle; wouldn't you know it—was out.

Slowly Susan moved her hand toward her handbag. Berry lifted her gun. A smile slowly spread over her face—an evil gloating smile. This is it, Susan thought. Curtains for Susan Melville. NOTED ARTIST SLAIN ON DEPARTMENT STORE ESCALATOR. What a way to die.

There was a cough. "Pardon me." An elderly man in tweeds popped up at Berry's elbow. "Could you tell me where the sporting goods are?"

Berry's mouth worked but no sound came out. The elderly man brought his mouth close to her ear. "I said, 'Do you know where the sporting goods are?' " he bellowed, in a voice calculated to penetrate even the most obdurate eardrum.

Berry regained a measure of control. "No need to yell. I'm not deaf. And I have no idea where the sporting goods are."

"Then why are you standing there waving a gun about?"

Berry looked down at the gun in her hand as if she didn't know how it had gotten there. "Oh, this isn't a gun. It's a—a cigarette lighter."

Those seemed to be the magic words. Suddenly the area in front of the escalator was filled with store personnel. "Smoking is not allowed in the store," said an authoritative young woman.

"It's against the law," said an equally authoritative young man. "On the other hand, it is permitted in all of our restaurants."

"Sorry sir," said a middle-aged woman, "but Bloomingdale's does not have a sporting goods department." She turned to Berry. "However it does have a department of clothes for the full-figured woman, which is located on the Metro level."

Berry gave her a suspicious look. "What's the Metro level?"

The escalator decanted Susan right in front of Berry. The two ladies glared at one another. "The Metro level is the basement," Susan informed her. "And 'full-figured' means 'queen-sized.' In other words, fat."

All three Bloomingdale employees paled. "Bloomingdale's has no basements," the authoritative young woman declared.

"And we never use the word 'fat'," the middle-aged woman added.

All three kept their eyes fixed on Berry. She put the gun back in her handbag. Susan moved to the side, out of earshot of the Bloomingdale bunch. She indicated with her head that Berry was to follow her, which Berry did with the utmost reluctance.

"I don't know why you want to kill me," Susan said in a low voice. "I've never done anything to you."

"Never done anything!" Berry's voice rose. "*Never done anything*! Do you call ruining my life nothing?"

"Shhh, we're attracting attention."

Berry lowered her voice, probably recollecting that this was not Gandistan, and it was wiser not to engage openly in heated argument with someone whom you were planning to kill shortly. "You came between Buck and me. Do you know, I never saw him again after that time you interfered!"

Susan was glad to know it. She had never been sure.

"He told me on the phone that it would be too dangerous for us ever to meet again now that you knew about us. I begged and pleaded but he said no, it was all over, but he would treasure my memory forever. I've hated you ever since."

Her face swelled with the effort, she was making to keep her voice down. "And you've hated me, because you were jealous. You wanted

175

him all to yourself. You had an Electra complex, or whatever they call it now."

"They don't call it anything, because there isn't any such thing—at least not any more."

"Of course, you'd say that. But it's true."

"You're crazy, do you know that? Mad as a hatter. Besides, I don't hate you. I merely dislike you more than words can say."

"People don't try to kill each other just because they dislike them. And I know you came here to kill me—no use denying it."

"I'm not denying it. People do kill other people who are threatening to kill them, and you threatened to kill me if I didn't join the Rundle House board. What else can I do? Besides, you're a menace to society."

Berry's voice was incredulous. "You want to kill me because you think I'm a menace to society? And you call *me* crazy!"

The authoritative young man approached them. "Pardon me, ladies, but I'm afraid you're blocking traffic. If you could just move to some other part of the store. The restaurants are open for breakfast," he added.

"I'm so sorry, I didn't realize we were in the way," Susan said. Berry looked as if she were going to spit at him.

He backed away from them. The two ladies backed away from each other, like a pair of cats with uncertain territorial imperatives. Once she was sure she was well out of range of Berry's gun, Susan began to turn; then wheeled, in case this was some kind of feint on Berry's part.

But, no, she was walking away as briskly as she could—rather, waddling away. She'd had sense enough not to wear stilt heels for the occasion, but even two-inch heels were too high for her to manage a rapid getaway.

Seen from behind, she was even more outlandish than from in front, and an above-the-knee skirt, however fashionable, was simply wrong for someone with knees like hers. There seemed to be some sort of sticker on the back of her stole with a printed legend on it that Susan was too far away to be able to read. "Plain old Berry Rundle," Susan thought, was a lot more conspicuous than the Begum in full regalia.

SUSAN WENT OVER to the bank of elevators, which fronted upon a long, deserted corridor—a good place for a shootout, she thought, as she glanced warily at both ends. Since she appeared to be alone for the moment, she took the opportunity to remove her jacket, take out her gun, and drape the jacket over it.

She pressed the elevator button with her free hand. She felt more confident now. Whichever came first, the elevator or Berry, she was ready for either.

The elevator came first. Going up. Up was as good as down, especially since she had no idea where Berry might be. Hadn't she said something about needing to buy glasses? The "Main Course"—china, glassware, housewares—was on the sixth floor, Susan recalled. She decided to make that her destination. If she did not find Berry there, she would take the elevator back down, floor by floor. Anyone riding down on an escalator made too good a target.

There were only two passengers in the elevator. One was a middle-aged woman who gave the usual stony stare to the newcomer. The other was the young man who had been following Berry.

Susan pretended not to recognize him. He appeared not to recognize her. Perhaps he really didn't recognize her. He couldn't have seen her coming down the escalator. He might not even know what she looked like. It all depended on whether he had been at the trustees' tea or not.

She got off at the sixth floor. The young man remained on the elevator. Either he was going to bedding and linen on seven or whatever it was they had on eight; she couldn't remember. Or he didn't know where he was going. He looked as if he didn't know where he was going.

THERE WERE SO many fragile objects on the sixth floor that navigation was hazardous, complicated by the fact that there were so many mirrors around. Even the wariest shopper ran the risk of either crashing into a mirror or into a delicate display. There weren't too many people around; and they were visible sometimes as themselves, sometimes as reflections. But neither reality nor reflection wore purple, so, unless Berry was a quick-change artist or lurking somewhere behind a partition or in the corridor off which the elevators opened, she was not on the sales floor.

Susan walked past an army of arcane kitchen gadgets that would have had Michelle drooling, over to the escalators. Banks of TV screens were promoting a special purchase of Ruritanian crystal in insinuating continental accents. She looked down to the fifth floor, while trying to keep an alert eye behind her—not as difficult as it might seem, because she

177

was bound to see a purple flash in the mirrors if Berry were suddenly to appear.

All she could see below was furniture. No sign of Berry downstairs (down-escalator?) unless she was hiding behind that overstuffed couch. For a moment Susan thought she saw Berry peering out between the shelves of an étagère—but, no, it was only a large and particularly hideous Toby jug.

She knew that looking for Berry in Bloomingdale's was like looking for the proverbial needle (notions) in a haystack (beauty salon). Her confidence was beginning to ebb. You could be lost in Bloomingdale's for days and no one would find you. The only reason she felt she had any chance of finding Berry was that she knew Berry would be looking for her.

She was not going to give up now. She would proceed in her quest. The next step would be to check the fifth floor on its own level. She started to head in the direction of the elevators; almost walked into a mirror which was reflecting the area in which she thought she was going; swerved and came within a hair's-breadth of colliding with a table full of Chinese rice bowls.

"Susie!" a voice called out behind her. "Susie! I been lookin' all over the store for ya!"

She turned. There was the Bat, Carlo Battaglia, C. Montague himself, with a burly man on either side of him. In fact, there were two Bats, with four burly men. Behind them she could see two hangdog young men carrying cellular telephones; no, four hangdog young men with four cellular telephones; and, if she looked in the wrong direction, an infinite number of hangdog young men carrying cellular telephones.

She didn't know which were real and which were reflections. She didn't care. Whichever they were, they were in her way. If only they would all prove to be illusory and vanish.

No such luck. "I thought I'd give you two ladies a surprise and join ya," the Bat beamed. "I wanted to look over the place before I made 'em an offer, so I says to myself what better way to do it than in such classy company."

"So that's why he was following me," Susan said, gesturing at Nicky —or was it Nicky's reflection? Whichever it was turned red and stumbled into a display of huge copper pots which clanged but did not topple. The Bat frowned. "You wanted to know where in the store we were going to be?"

"I tole him not to letcha see him," the Bat said. "But even if you din't, you were bound to smell him. Phew, he stinks to high heaven!"

Nicky sounded near tears. "I cooden help it. A lady downstairs sprayed it on me. And it isn't a stink; it's the latest in fashionable masculine scents. She give me a little card that says so. See!"

The Bat shook his head. "I'm afraid Nicky's not good for much. Not that Tony's much better."

Tony gave a nervous leap. A tray of crystal goblets swayed and shattered.

The display might be a reflection, but the crash was real. A saleswoman strode toward them, blood in her eye.

"He let the queen chase him away, but at least he saw ya in the elevator and tipped me off where ya were heading. Well, whadda you want?"

The saleswoman opened her mouth, but seemed incapable of speech. She pointed to the smashed crystal.

The Bat waved his hand. "Oh, that! I'll take care of it." He reached into his breast pocket.

Good heavens, Susan thought, he's going for his gun. If he shoots her, the store will be filled with police. All my plans will go down the drain.

But all the Bat brought out was a charge card. "Put it on my tab," he said.

The saleswoman accepted it frostily. The store might forgive him but she had her reservations. She retired with the card to the secret recesses of the store to do whatever it was salespeople did with charge cards.

Susan was surprised to find that card-carrying members of the Mafia were also card-carrying members of American Express or Master Charge. No reason why she should have been, she thought, upon reflection. You could get a credit card as long as you could establish a good credit record—by fair means or foul. Good character didn't enter into it.

"Well, that's taken care of," the Bat said. "An' it's gonna come out of your salary," he said to the miserable Tony. "Teach you to be more graceful."

He turned back to Susan. "You're lookin' real good, Susie. Don't forget we're steppin' out tomorrow so put on your gladdest rags."

The bewilderment must have shown on her face. "You haven't forgotten our dinner date for tomorrow night?"

"How could I forget?" As a matter of fact she had forgotten, though "blocked it out" might be the more apt phrase. Having dinner with him was going to be awkward. Perhaps she could call it off under what she hoped would be the circumstances. If things didn't turn out the way she hoped, there would be no need for her to worry. It would be called off automatically.

"So what have you done with the queen?" the Bat demanded jovially.

She couldn't help a nervous start. "Nothing yet. What I mean is, we seem to have gotten separated. I was just going to look for her. When I last saw her she was on the third floor. Maybe she's still there."

"Well, le's go look for her together," the Bat said, offering her his arm, only it was her reflection to which he made the gesture. He laughed. "This store's like a fun house. I like it, I like it."

Susan certainly didn't want the Bat to accompany her while she flushed Berry out of whatever covert she might have gone to earth in. "She did say something about going to the ladies' room. It could be embarrassing if we all went down there, especially after what happened when Nicky was waiting outside the ladies' room."

The Bat frowned. "What did happen?"

Nicky gave Susan a reproachful glance. "Nuthin' happened," he said. "I jus' knocked over a rack of clothes. They weren't breakable or anythin'."

"Oh, Nicky, Nicky," the Bat sighed, "sometimes I think I shoulda let you go to cookin' school, the way your Mama wanted."

"Why don't I go see if Berry's in the ladies' room," Susan said, "and, if I find her, I'll bring her back up here."

Without waiting for the Bat's reply, she started toward the corridor off which the elevators opened. Behind her she could hear him saying something, but, as she was turning the corner, she couldn't make out the actual words.

An elevator door opened. Berry burst out. "So there you are! Enough of this playing hide-and-seek all round the store. My feet hurt. I'm going to finish you off once and for all." There was a gun in her hand.

Susan backed away from the elevator corridor. She lifted her gun. From the angle at which Berry was pointing her gun, Susan saw that it was her reflection at which Berry was aiming, not Susan herself.

But there were no mirrors behind Berry. It was Berry, the real, live Berry in the considerable flesh, at whom Susan was pointing her gun.

"Ladies, ladies . . . !" the Bat's voice said, close behind her. Very close behind. He sounded alarmed, as well he might.

Susan and Berry fired at the same time. Susan's gun hit its mark. Berry crumpled to the ground. But not before her bullet had hit a mark —but not the one she intended.

There was a loud cry, followed by a thud. Susan did not turn to see whom Berry's bullet had hit, but she had a suspicion it had been the Bat.

AN ELEVATOR DOOR opened just ahead. She went toward it, circling Berry's body. The fur stole lay across the purple silk like a banner. She could read the sticker on the stole now. "Animals have rights, too," it said. Well, she wasn't going to argue with that.

Inside the elevator two ladies dressed in the height of fashion were carrying on an animated conversation. They ignored Susan's entrance. They ignored the screams and the sound of further gunshots as the doors closed behind her. They ignored the people who entered as the elevator stopped, time after time, on its maddeningly slow crawl to the ground floor.

Susan left, trying to look as if she were part of a group. Passing a clump of people who were waiting for the elevator to go up (was that Andy Mackay she glimpsed among them or was it just another illusion?), she moved as swiftly as she could, consonant with a decorous shopping pace, toward the front doors and the street.

As she came out, she could hear the sound of sirens approaching. No time to stop and try to get a cab. She walked up Lexington Avenue until she had covered six blocks or so, far enough to take her away from the scene. She was about to hail a taxi when she asked herself: why take a taxi on a fine day like this? She would walk back home. She had plenty of time now.

XXVII

MICHELLE WAS SURPRISED and not at all pleased to see her employer return so soon. "Thought you was gonna be out a lot longer'n this."

"My business didn't take as long as I expected, so I thought I might as well make my calls from here," Susan said, wondering why she felt this compulsion to explain to Michelle, when it should be Michelle who explained to her—and there was plenty that needed explaining. "Have you done the shopping yet?"

"I ain't had no time, okay? I don't think you realize how much there is to do around here."

"Good, because there are a few more things I want you to get. And you'd better go get them now, because I am going to have lunch at home. Maybe even dinner. I'm exhausted."

"But you were on'y gone an hour. What were y'doin'—weight-liftin'?"

"Something like that," Susan said. Lifting a weight off her mind, anyway.

As soon as Michelle had gone, Susan turned on the radio to see if news of the shootout in Bloomingdale's had reached the airwaves. It had, but accounts were sketchy and confused. There seemed, according to a bemused-sounding WINS announcer, to have been a gang war in Bloomingdale's. Carlo Battaglia, also known as "the Bat," head of the Puzzone crime family had been shot to death, and so had a well-dressed middle-aged woman whose identity had not as yet been established. Several of his henchmen had been seriously wounded in the battle, and a female member of the sales staff had been grazed by a bullet.

She had to call the Waldorf fast, Susan thought, and explain why she apparently hadn't shown up at Bloomingdale's, before Berry's body was identified. She had her story ready. She would ask for the Begum. Obviously the Begum would not be there. Then she would ask for the king. If the police had already found out who Berry was, he wasn't likely to be accessible. However, if she did reach him, she would tell him that she had gone to Bloomingdale's and found the place cordoned off by the police. It was obvious, she would say, that something had happened, possibly a bomb threat. Department stores were always getting bomb threats. Probably Berry hadn't been able to get in, either, but, in case she had arrived early, Susan wanted her to know that she hadn't been stood up.

However, she couldn't reach Serwar, so she had to table her story for later. On the whole, she was relieved not to have to talk to him right then. It would be hard to talk to someone whose mother you have just killed, while pretending that you had no idea she was dead.

Later, after Berry had been identified, Susan would call Serwar with her condolences. Or he might call her to give her the news himself. Other people would call, too. Andy, without question. Probably Lucy, and, of course, the rest of "the old gang," as Berry had termed them. She hoped she wouldn't be invited to the funeral. If it took place in New York, she was very much afraid she would be. And she would have to attend, no way out of it.

She probably wouldn't be invited to the Bat's funeral, but she would send flowers. After all, he had sent her flowers. She felt a twinge of regret and wasn't sure whether it was because the Bat was dead or because she hadn't been the one to kill him.

THE PHONE RANG. She picked it up, prepared to greet the news of Berry's death with, first incredulity, then shock. But it was nobody connected with the late Begum. It was Ralph Towers, the young man from the Foundation.

"Miss Melville, I've been trying to reach you for some time. I'm afraid I have bad news."

He paused, apparently to give her a chance to steel herself. If the events of the morning haven't steeled me, she thought, nothing would. "It's about Peter, isn't it?"

"I'm afraid so. Dr. Franklin and a companion went off on a side trip some weeks ago. When they didn't come back, a search was organized. Nobody could find any traces of them."

Susan was silent, wondering how she felt.

"That doesn't mean all hope is lost, of course. There weren't any signs of any kind of—uh—accident or anything. But I thought you should be prepared for the—that you should be prepared."

"That's very kind of you," she said. "Very thoughtful. Who was this companion who disappeared along with him? Anyone I know?"

"Katherine Froehlich. She used to work at the Foundation."

Dr. Froehlich! So Susan's suspicions had been true. It looked as if Peter had taken one side trip too many.

Mr. Towers interpreted her silence as an inability to speak because of grief. "If there's anything I can do . . . ?"

"Just keep me posted. I'm sure it'll all turn out to be some kind of a mistake. Peter and Dr. Froehlich must simply have gone off in an entirely different direction from the one they were supposed to be taking. Or they left the country without telling anyone. Peter's always so careless about forwarding addresses. They're bound to turn up safe and sound sooner or later."

"Of course they are," he said. "May I say you're being very brave, Miss Melville?"

She was tempted to reply, "No, you may not, Mr. Towers," but she controlled herself. "Let's keep in touch," she said.

AFTER HE'D HUNG up, she sat for a while, trying to analyze *her* emotions. She was naturally sorry that Peter had disappeared and was presumably dead. At the same time, she was less sorry than she might have been if he'd had a companion other than Dr. Froehlich.

Susan and Peter had been together for many years now, and, although she had found her impatience with him growing over the years, that was true of most couples she knew. Odd, she reflected, that she had never thought of Peter and herself as a couple before.

Mimi Von Schwabe, of course, dealt with the problem of having a relationship grow stale by changing spouses—for she was always in a state of marriage—from time to time. She had stayed with Gunther Von Schwabe longer than most of her previous husbands because, she told Susan, it was time she settled down. But Susan knew that Gunther had said, "If ever my Mimmchen tries to leave me for another man, I will strangle her with my own hands. And also him."

Susan picked up the phone and dialed Mimi's number. "Mimi," she said, after they had gotten through the usual amenities, "do you remember when I was at your house for dinner a couple of weeks ago? There was a young artist sitting next to me. I'm afraid I don't remember his name. I promised I'd introduce him to some sympathetic gallery owners."

Mimi said she'd given so many dinners with so many young artists as guests she'd forgotten which one Susan was referring to. Susan resisted the impulse to ask her for a list of all of them. "Oh, I'm so sorry, Mimi," she said. "I know what a wretched memory you have. Perhaps Gunther will remember. I saw his face when you and that young man—whatever his name was—came in after that long conversation you had on the terrace. I'm sure Gunther will be able to tell me what his name was."

There was no point in bothering Gunther with such a triviality, Mimi said. He was a diplomat; he had more important things on his mind. She was sure that, if she thought hard, she would be able to supply Susan with the young man's name.

"Think hard, then," Susan said.